DEEP CUT

THE DEEP SERIES - BOOK TWO

NICK SULLIVAN

Cover design by Shayne Rutherford of Wicked Good Book Covers
Cover island photo provided by Cees Timmers and the Saba Board of Tourism
Cover airplane photo provided by Rolf Jonsen and PlanePics.org
Copy editing by Marsha Zinberg of The Write Touch
Proofreading by Sondra Wolfer and Gretchen Tannert Douglas
Interior Design and Typesetting by Colleen Sheehan of Ampersand Book Interiors
Original maps by Rainer Lesniewski/Shutterstock.com

ISBN: 978-0-9978132-4-1

Published by Wild Yonder Press
www.WildYonderPress.com

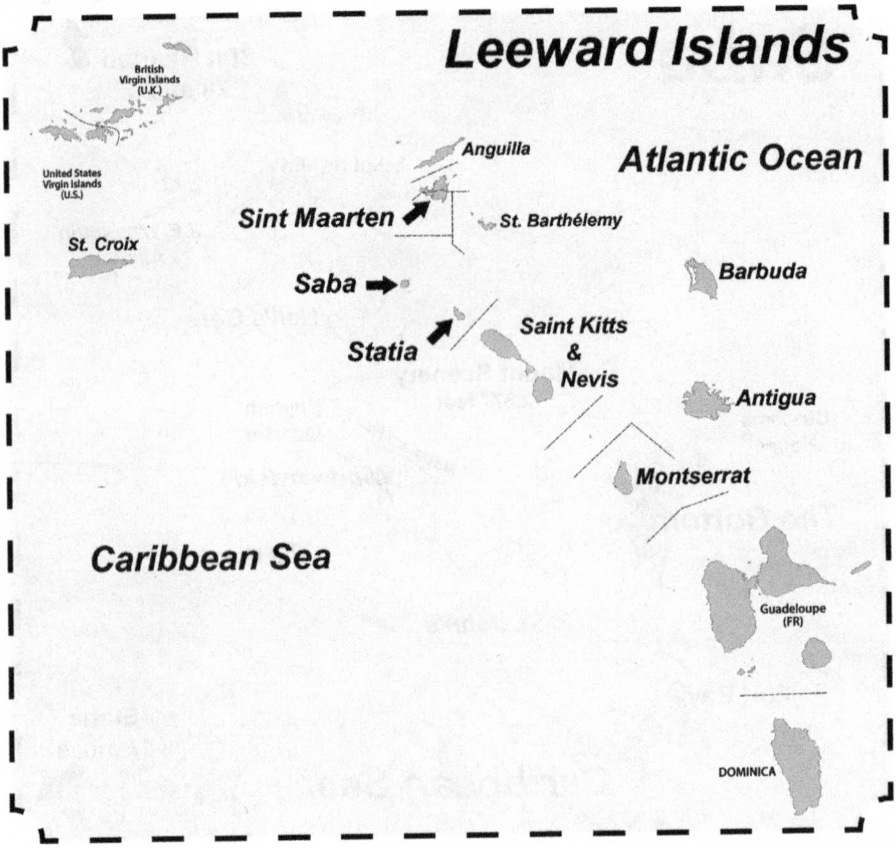
Leeward Islands
British
Virgin Islands
(U.K.)
United States
Virgin Islands
(U.S.)
St. Croix
Anguilla
Atlantic Ocean
Sint Maarten
St. Barthélemy
Saba
Barbuda
Statia
Saint Kitts
&
Nevis
Antigua
Montserrat
Caribbean Sea
Guadeloupe
(FR)
DOMINICA

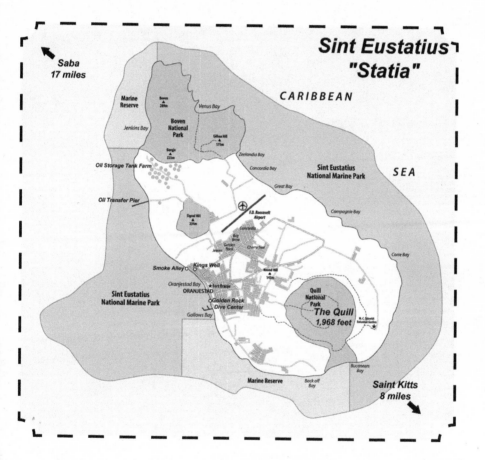

*To all the good people of Saba who gave me
their time, their knowledge, and their stories.*

1

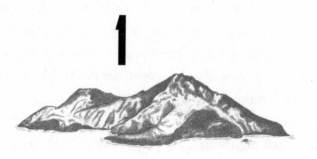

August 27, 2017

"Time is it?" mumbled a voice, filtered through a pillow.

"No idea," the young man replied.

Emily Durand sighed and rolled faceup. "Guess we just stay in bed forever then. Nothing like a lazy lie-in."

Boone Fischer swung his long legs over the side of the bed and rose to his feet, wincing a bit at various aches and pains sustained from the day before ... as well as a few newer ones from last night. Those he didn't mind so much. He stretched, his wiry arms nearly brushing the ceiling of the little cottage. "I'll go check ol' Mister Sun," he said through a yawn. "See what he's got to say about the time."

"How very caveman of you." Emily giggled and sat up in the bed, the sheet slipping partway from her body. "But since when is the sun a bloke?"

Boone held up a hand. "I'm gonna need some coffee before I can engage you in witty banter…" His eyes dipped down from her face before flicking back to her green eyes. One side of her lips quirked up in a knowing half-smile. Boone blew out a breath, shaking his head with a grin. He approached the floor-length curtains they'd drawn across the exit to the balcony and slid them swiftly to the side. Brilliant sunlight flooded the room.

Emily hissed in a half-hearted imitation of a sun-scorched vampire, pulling the sheet over her head. "Mister Sun is a prat," said the lump under the sheet.

Boone laughed and plucked Emily's lime green sunglasses from the nightstand, popping them onto the head of the ghost in the bed. "Here. You've been without these for hours. Probably suffering from withdrawal."

As Emily dropped the sheet from her face and slid the shades on, Boone felt strangely comforted. He'd gotten to know Em through their work at a Bonaire dive shop, and this girl he'd fallen for was rarely without her sunglasses during daylight hours. He grabbed a pair of shorts off the back of a chair. "Looks like it's about one o'clock. I'm not sure if the other cabins have a view of *this* cabin, so…" He pulled on the shorts and headed onto the balcony to take in the spectacular view.

Under an azure blue sky, the cottage was surrounded by bright flowers and lush greenery. Looking straight out to the south over the tops of red-roofed homes and sloping cliffs, he could see the turquoise seas of the Caribbean stretched to the horizon, throwing up occasional sparkles from the sun high overhead. The Dutch island of Saba was essentially a mountain in the ocean, and here at the El Momo cottages atop Booby Hill, they were over 1,600 feet above sea level. A low whistle came from beside Boone.

"The sunset was nice and all, but this is ace!" Emily was wrapped in the sheet from the bed, her face shining with wonder. "We should go exploring!"

Boone looked down at her. Emily Durand was just under five feet tall and her makeshift cloak billowed across the deck, completely obscuring her feet. "How many different ways are you gonna wear that sheet?" Boone laughed, pulling her to him.

"You don't like it ... get rid of it." She bit her lower lip, a look of mischief playing across her features.

Boone pressed against her and started to lean in for a kiss but stopped abruptly, snorting a laugh.

"What?" Emily's tone was halfway between amused and offended.

"Your sunglasses ... my reflection ... it's like I'm leaning in to kiss myself."

"Then close your eyes, you berk." She reached up and grabbed the back of his head, pulling him down to her lips.

Boone kissed her deeply but forced himself to withdraw when their breathing began to quicken. "Em, much as I'd like to snog all day with you—"

Emily burst into laughter. "*Snog*? You stealing my slang, Tennessee boy?"

"What can I say? You're infectious."

Emily made a face. "*Infectious* ... oh, you smooth talker, you. While we're chatting lingo, I probably should teach you the difference between 'snogging' and 'shagging.' Lesson One: we've been doing both."

Boone grinned and held up his hands in surrender. "Look, I know Scenery Scuba said they'd give me a couple extra days before I start, but there's still things I need to do. I should hit the

"Tricia the Trip!" Rodney crowed. "Trish is the Queen of Martini Night."

"Make sure you stop by on Thursdays," Amber said. "This week it's Passion Fruit Martinis."

"Sign me up!" Emily proclaimed.

"Hey, Rodney, how's Sid doing?" Boone asked. "He was pretty banged up. Figure we should go see him."

"I heard he cracked a couple ribs but he should be all right. Think he's at his girlfriend's house, down in The Bottom."

"It's a beautiful day," Emily remarked. "Maybe we can walk down there, pay him a visit?"

Rodney shook his head. "You *could*, but I wouldn't recommend it. Saba may be only five square miles, but a lot of that is steep slopes. I've got an airport pickup at five but I can run you down to The Bottom after. I'll call you on Anders's phone when I'm back up top."

"Sounds like a plan," Boone said as Amber offered them menus.

———◆·◆———

After a quick lunch they decided to walk around town until Rodney called them. Down the street from Scout's they came to a T-intersection.

"This looks familiar," Emily said. "When Rodney ran us down to the port, right?"

"Yeah, this is The Road. He nodded to the left. "That way's The Bottom and Fort Bay. We go the other way, you'll hit Hell's Gate, and then the airport."

"I still can't get over that landing. Like flying straight at a cliff and then plopping down to stop on a dime. Hey, speaking of the airport, there's the fella who gave us a ride up."

Across the road, a dapper older man in khakis and a tweed vest over a crisp, white shirt was exiting a little building with a sign over the door reading *Saba Snack*. Carrying what looked like a vanilla milkshake, he was taking a long pull on a straw, a look of ecstasy on his face.

"Hey, Gordon!" Boone called out.

Gordon Hollenbeck stopped mid-sip and squinted across the road before making his way to their side. "Well, fancy meeting you two! I hear you had quite the day of it yesterday. You know, you're lucky to see me out and about on a lazy Sunday, with all the grocery stores and half the restaurants closed, but I heard the soursop crop had come in and I just had to get a smoothie." Gordon spoke with a breezy, theatrical air and Boone remembered the little man had said he'd been a dresser on Broadway.

"What's soursop?" Boone asked.

"Oh ... delightful fruit, spiky and green on the outside, creamy and white on the inside. It grows in a few places up on the mountain and it's only available for a month or two. The owner here calls it by the Spanish name, *guanábana*."

"What's it taste like?"

"You tell me." He removed the lid and offered the drink for each to take a sip.

"Whoa ... tastes like strawberries and pineapple," Emily gushed.

"I was gonna say mango and banana," Boone said. "A little tart, too."

Gordon snatched it back. "And the fruit itself—the flesh is soft and custardy ... nothing like it! Well, enough about fruit. Have you moved into your new abode?"

"Well, that door looks pretty rickety. And besides, the girl who works there takes the cash box with her when she locks up. There's nothing in there to steal but T-shirts and hats."

"Or maps," Boone said to himself, remembering the bundle of papers the man had tossed into the SUV.

"Most of the trail maps are online or free at the Tourism Office," Gordon said. "No, I imagine that lock's been broken for a while."

"Hold on, fellas," Emily broke in. "How about clueing me in, yeah?"

"Sorry," Boone said. "It was just some…guy. Something seemed off about him, but I dunno… after everything that's happened over the past few days, I'm probably expecting threats where there aren't any."

A cell phone rang and Boone jumped. Reaching down to a cargo pocket, he removed the envelope Amber had given him and extracted Anders's phone. "Hello?"

"Boone, this is Rodney. I've finished my drop-off. You still want to head down to see Sid?"

"Now more than ever," Boone responded. Sidney Every was a police "aspirant," the Dutch equivalent of a rookie cop, and might want to look into a potential break-in.

"All right. Where can I pick you two up?"

"We're by the trail shop."

"It's closed," Rodney said helpfully.

"Sort of," Boone replied.

2

*S**tupid, stupid, stupid!*

The man savagely gripped the wheel of the SUV as he made another hairpin turn on The Road. Far below, the red-and-white buildings of Saba's capital, The Bottom, stretched across his driver's side window.

It had been a simple plan: stop by the shop—just another guy looking to do a hike who didn't know about the Sunday hours—then pop the lock, grab the maps, drive away. But the mountain had called to him and he had hesitated. And then that *voice*. That beautiful, feminine laugh, so full of life...

You've already laid the groundwork to get what you need. Anything else is a distraction. On to the next phase. You have your maps.

The man reached across to the passenger seat and fanned them out. Some of the maps were very old and worn, torn at their folds. Others were photocopies of surveyor's maps. The tourist trail maps simply didn't have the detail he needed, and he had guessed correctly that they might have something more "professional" tucked away in the trail shop. These were ideal for his purposes.

A soft horn toot from below alerted him to an oncoming car approaching the blind curve on the switchback ahead. He eased his vehicle a little more to the right as he approached the Midway Bar, snugging his ball cap further down over his sunglasses. A small yellow car rounded the bend, ascending, an elderly lady at the wheel. The man raised a lazy hand in greeting as she passed, and it was no accident that his casual wave rose to a point that obscured his face. Minutes later he reached the Saba Medical School on the edge of town before curving around an ancient-looking church and coming to a T-intersection. The Saba Police Station sat squarely in front of him. Hunching over, he quickly turned left and headed for the northwestern edge of town called The Gap, passing the hospital before heading up Ladder Road.

This little street was ideal, with just seven houses along its entire length, only some of which were currently occupied. An eighth house was in the early stages of construction and that was where he pulled in now. He had learned that the owner, a man from the States, had passed away, and the skeleton of the building now sat bare, the roof only partially completed. Popping the hatchback, he removed a couple of industrial buckets and a few tools, setting them against the rear of the SUV to give it the appearance of a workman's truck. Satisfied, he stepped back from the vehicle and raised his eyes to the east.

Rising above the nearby ridge, Mount Scenery dominated the sky, the immense stratovolcano filling his view. The cloud cover that frequently shrouded its summit had burned off and he could make out the tall communications tower that crowned its nearly 3,000-foot height. A rush of euphoria flooded his mind and body.

So beautiful. So … powerful. Soon. Very soon.

Looking toward the sea, he noted the orange hues beginning to infuse themselves into the sky. The sun would set in less than an hour. Reaching into the back, he retrieved the case of water he'd picked up earlier from Saba Wishes, the only supermarket with Sunday hours. Closing the hatchback, he listened intently for any cars and was greeted with the silence he expected, this being one of the sleepiest roads on the island. He hefted the water bottles and headed toward the unfinished house. Unlike most cottages on Saba, this one had a substantial basement.

3

As Rodney Hassell's taxi van made its winding way down the slopes of Saba, Emily glanced back from the passenger's seat and watched Boone. He had been unusually quiet since leaving Windwardside. While Rodney had chattered away happily and Emily bantered right back, Boone had sat in the back, occasionally laughing at one of her jokes or asking Rodney a question. Now, as they neared The Bottom, Boone seemed to be deep in thought, silently staring at his feet. Sunset was less than an hour away and already the sky behind the pair of hills to the west was rimmed in fiery colors.

"Earth to Boone. Beautiful vistas can be yours for the low, low price of a slight turn of the head … … unless the back of Rodney's car seat is doing it for you."

Boone raised his eyes. "Sorry. Woolgathering, as my mom would say."

"What, your mum sheared sheep?"

Boone looked confused for a second, then burst into laughter. Emily smiled and turned back around. *That's better. There's my*

Boone. But then again, if she was honest with herself, this lanky man did have an introspective side that could crank itself up to eleven from time to time. He'd clearly gotten the heebie-jeebies back there, and while it was true that coming off a few days of fighting terrorists would set any sane person on edge, Boone seemed to have a knack for picking up on things most people would never sense.

She remembered two separate incidents on dive boats while working at Rock Beauty Divers in Bonaire. In one instance, he'd taken Emily aside and asked her to keep a sharp eye on a woman whose dive log indicated she was a veteran diver. They'd been diving with her for several days and she seemed highly competent, but Emily had promised she'd keep her in sight. Once they were at depth, the diver had suffered a panic attack and Em had been right by her side to calm her down and slowly bring her up to fifteen feet for a safety stop.

Another time, on a two-tank boat dive, he had gotten a vibe off a solo diver who had complained about ear problems and sat out the first dive, remaining aboard with the boat's captain. During the surface interval the man said he'd sit out the second dive as well, heading up the ladder to the flybridge to take a nap. Emily watched Boone look up at the man for a moment, then go below, saying he needed to fix a piece of gear before they hit the water. After the second dive, as the boat was heading back to Kralendijk, Boone retrieved something from near the water cooler and motioned for Emily to join him on the flybridge alongside the skipper. He produced a paper cup with his name written in Sharpie—it was common practice on dive boats to label a single cup and try to use it throughout your stay to cut down on trash. Emily noticed the cup had a hole cut into the side, concealed in one of the O's in Boone's name. Boone reached in and withdrew the tiny GoPro he used from time to time. He explained he'd removed it from the watertight case and adjusted the video to a lower resolution so it could run throughout their dive, then set the cup over by the cooler. They leaned in as he pressed the play button: the image showed one of the benches back in the sheltered portion of the cockpit, opposite the water cooler. There was a pile of three or four dry bags that a group of Floridians had placed there, out of the sun and spray. Boone fast-forwarded the video and fifteen minutes into the dive, Mr. "My-ears-are-giving-me-trouble" entered the frame and quickly went through the dry bags, extracting money from two wallets he found within. The captain cursed and picked up his cell phone. By the time the boat reached the shore, the Bonaire police were waiting on the dock.

"Here we are," Rodney said, snapping Emily from her reverie. He pulled alongside a low wall below a tidy Saban cottage. A little wooden sign read *Island Thyme* in green lettering. "This is Sophie's place. She'll be inside playing nursemaid to Sid, I 'spect. She can probably run you back to El Momo, but I'll be back at Scout's if you need me."

As Rodney drove away down the narrow backstreet, Boone and Emily stepped onto the porch of the little cottage. The inner door was open and Emily could hear voices inside. She rapped a knuckle against the screen door frame.

"One moment," came a feminine voice, and a tall woman with caramel skin came into view, swinging open the screen door. "You must be Boone and Emily," she said, her voice rich with a light island singsong. "Rodney said you'd be by. I'm Sophie Leven-stone." Emily couldn't help notice the woman's eyes lingering on Boone a moment longer than she would have preferred. Not that she could blame her. Tall and sculpted with lean muscle without an ounce of fat, Boone was a striking man. Sophie's eyes met

Emily's and she smiled broadly. "Come in, please. Sid's on the couch there, pretending to be hurt."

"Oh, come on, Sofe. You're the one treating me like I broke my neck," Sidney Every said from a rattan-framed sofa in the far corner. Over his head were a number of watercolors depicting a progression of vistas, identical except for the position of the sun. The room was lit by soft light from a pair of floor lamps, and the gentle hum of a ceiling fan pulsed against Emily's ears. Sid waggled a bottle of Heineken at the pair. "Can I offer you two a beer? Figure I owe you one."

"Sure," Boone said. "Heineken? Aren't we on a tropical isle?"

"We're on a tropical *Dutch* isle. I'll have you know, Saba is one of the highest per capita consumers of Heineken in the world."

"Not sure that's something to brag about, Sid," Sophie said with a smile. "Emily, how about you?"

Emily gave a thumbs up, turning to Sid as Sophie left for the kitchen. "You're not on painkillers?" Emily asked.

"Just ibuprofen. Two ribs had hairline fractures—nothing too serious. I'm on modified duty for a few days. They're going to put me in the police annex in Windwardside."

"Further away from me," Sophie said wistfully, returning with a pair of Heinekens.

"Oh, come on. You spend half your time posted at the airport."

"Are you a pilot?" Emily asked, taking a beer and plopping into a matching rattan seat alongside the sofa.

"Funny you should ask. I've been training for a pilot's certification but no, I'm with the fire department. Half our members are posted at the airport every day, but the main office is right here in The Bottom next to the police station. That's where I met Sid."

"And I'll never forget that day," Sid said, whistling and shaking his head.

"What, was it love at first sight?" Emily asked.

Sophie snorted a laugh and Sid blushed, hemming and hawing, "Umm ... no..." Sophie gasped in mock offense, and Sid continued, "Wait, I mean, *sure* it was! But..."

Sophie just laughed harder and Boone grinned, sitting in a cane chair. "Okay, this I gotta hear."

"Well..." Sid cleared his throat. "I was bringing in a suspect. Drunk and disorderly—the man had started a fight at a local house bar. He was very apologetic and came quietly so I made the mistake of not cuffing him. He was a friend of one of my squad mates and I figured I'd get him in a cell and let our mutual friend handle the booking. When I took him from the car, he rushed me..."

"He knocked you on your ass, as I recall," Sophie interjected.

"Yeah, yeah ... so, he makes a run for it around the back, toward the fire department. I follow, yelling for him to stop ... and Sophie stopped him. Oh, man, did she ever."

Emily leaned forward, looking up at the tall woman. "What did you do?"

Sophie shrugged. "A takedown. I *did* give him a chance to play nice."

Sid sat up and set his beer down on the glass-topped coffee table, a tremor of excitement in his voice. "Sofe here steps in front of the guy, holds a hand up in front of his face—the man grabs for her and ... and I *still* don't know exactly what she did—it happened so fast—but the guy was on the ground and gasping in the blink of an eye. She even held him in an arm lock while I got the cuffs on him."

Sophie reached down and ran a hand through Sid's hair. "I'd seen Sid around the station and thought he was cute—been wondering how I could get him to notice me."

Sid laughed. "I'd *already* noticed you, you know that. You were just showing off."

"Maybe a little," Sophie said, smiling as she took a swig from her beer.

"What's your style?" Boone asked.

Sophie looked at Boone over the bottle. "Krav Maga. I lived in Sint Maarten for a while and trained at a studio there."

"Is that some kind of Caribbean martial art?" Emily asked.

"Oh, no, it's an Israeli combat style, developed by their military. Most of the indigenous Caribbean martial arts involve baton sticks or cutlasses."

"*Cutlasses?*" Boone spluttered. "What, like pirates?"

Sid laughed, "No, that's what Sabans call a machete."

"Boone here is into martial arts," Emily said. "He does that crazy dance karate … what is it, Boone? Caipirinha?" Emily raised her eyebrows at him, all innocence. She knew very well the name of the martial art he practiced, but she loved to "accidentally" confuse it with the popular Brazilian cocktail of cachaça, sugar, and lime.

Boone gave her a look before turning back to Sophie. "*Capoeira*. I also practice Brazilian Jiu-jitsu."

Sophie looked at Boone with focused interest. "I'm going to guess you're pretty good, aren't you?"

Boone shrugged. "Brown belt in jitsu. The capoeira … my teacher didn't really do rankings."

Emily knew Boone was being modest. One of the other dive instructors on Bonaire had told her that Boone was easily the equivalent of a black belt in both disciplines—he simply hadn't bothered to jump through some of the necessary hoops to officially rank. She was about to say so but stopped herself. Sophie seemed a bit *too* interested for her tastes. And the woman was statuesque and beautiful. *Jealous much, Em?* she thought to herself.

Sophie looked at Boone a moment longer before taking another sip from her beer and plopping down next to Sid. "I'd love to spar with you sometime," she said nonchalantly.

Sid didn't seem at all concerned with his girlfriend's offer. "Careful, Boone … or you'll wind up convalescing right beside me. She'll get you down on the ground and—"

"Say, Boone, did you want to tell Sid about that bloke that creeped you out?" Emily blurted. "And the broken lock?"

"What broken lock?" Sid asked, levity slipping from his face.

Boone quickly recounted his brief encounter with the stranger and the discovery of the broken hasp on the trail shop door. "Look, I didn't actually see the guy do anything wrong."

"And Gordon didn't recognize him? He seems to know everything about everyone on this island, so I'm thinking the man you saw was a tourist looking to go for a hike."

"How many tourists do you know who wear gray coveralls?"

Sid didn't have an answer for that. "Here's what I'll do … I'm going to be at the annex tomorrow morning; it's next door to Saba Snack, right up the street from the trail shop. I'll stop by as soon as they open and take a look, see if anything was taken."

"Have them check their maps," Boone said.

———— ◆ • ◆ ————

After a late dinner at Island Flavor in The Bottom, Sophie offered to take Boone and Emily back up to El Momo. Boone accepted and Emily immediately called shotgun. Once they were on their way, Boone leaned forward between the seats and asked numerous questions. On the twenty-minute ride, they learned several things about Sophie Levenstone. Both of her parents were seventh-generation Sabans and Sophie had grown up on the island, going to university in the States before spending some time on Sint Maarten, the Dutch portion of the dual French/Dutch island of Saint Martin. Her mother was a white Saban of Dutch descent and her father was of African descent. More importantly, *he* was a grandchild of the legendary Rebecca Levenstone.

"I never met her," Sophie said, "but every Saban knows the story of when my great-grandmother hauled a piano up The Ladder on her back."

"What's The Ladder?" Boone asked.

"There's a sheltered bay on the leeward side and before they built up Fort Bay, The Ladder was the only way to get goods and passengers ashore. You had to climb 800 steps, zig-zagging up to the customs house on the cliff, and then from there it was *still* a hike. You'll see that old, abandoned customs house a lot—it's above several of the popular dive sites. So, Rebecca was strong as an ox, and she would help the men unload the boats and bring the goods up The Ladder. More often than not she'd keep going, delivering things to people in the various villages."

"Hold on, back up a wee bit," Emily interjected. "She hauled a *piano* up 800 steps by herself?"

"That's the story," Sophie said. "My parents stick by it."

"Think you've inherited some of your great-grandma's super-strength?" Boone asked.

Sophie tossed a glance back over her shoulder. "Spar with me and find out."

"So, hey!" Emily broke in quickly. "That's cool … what's that?" She pointed at a little outcrop of buildings on a plateau to their right, the moonlit cliffs below it angling steeply toward the ocean.

"That's St. John's. Most of the schools for the island are there, except the big medical college in The Bottom."

"Can you climb down from there?" Emily asked. "To the sea?"

"Down the gut? Sure, you could make it down there, but it would be a hot hike back up. Oh, that kind of steep ravine? We call it a *gut*."

"Guts and cutlasses…" Boone mused. "We're not in Kansas anymore."

4

The next day, Boone wanted to get an early start moving in, so he bid the owner of El Momo farewell as the man called him a cab. Boone and Emily brought their luggage down the steps and were picked up by a cabbie named Garvis Hassell, a tall, lanky man who looked a bit like Anthony Bourdain. Emily asked if he was related to Rodney Hassell but Garvis, who was an eighth-generation Saban, explained that Hassell was the most common name on the island, with Johnson a close second. Just outside of Windwardside, the taxi pulled into a driveway on the left and Garvis announced they had arrived, dropping them off and motoring back onto The Road, heading down toward the airport.

As they pulled their luggage down the driveway, a tiny cottage came into view, the landscaping around it teeming with flowers. A tiny green sign with hand-painted lettering announced that this was *Hummingbird Haven*, and the name was justified in seconds as a shimmering hummingbird flitted by, coming to a hover by a stand of bright red heliconia. The cottage itself had the standard red roof and white walls, and numerous windows were framed in a dark green. A little flagstone path led around the side of the cottage, where a tiny outdoor seating area was set up just outside the front door. The view down the slopes to the Caribbean was breathtaking.

"Oh, Boone, I *love* it!"

"It's beautiful," Boone breathed. "Sure beats my little house in Rincon." Boone fished the key from the envelope to unlock the door, but Emily was already opening it.

"No crime, remember?"

Boone tucked the luggage just inside before heading back outdoors. "Let's take a stroll back to Windwardside."

"You don't want to put your stuff away?"

"Coffee first. Let's go back to town to grab some and hit the post office when they open."

"Ooh, I'd quite fancy a cuppa."

Boone looked at her askance. "Doesn't it mean 'tea' when you say cuppa?"

"Quit trying to suss my lingo, you half-Dutch Yank, for I am unfettered by the conventional norms of dialectic discourse," Emily intoned, letting her strong South London accent slip into a stuffy, professorial drone.

Boone grinned broadly at her. "That made no sense."

"You knew what I meant, yeah? So, it made sense. Now, let's go see if this island has decent coffee."

After a short walk back to Windwardside, they picked up some breakfast at a bakery and coffee shop called Bizzy B. Eva at El

Momo had recommended it. She might have been biased, seeing as she worked there from time to time, but as it turned out, the breakfast was delicious and the coffee was gratifyingly strong. They sat in a little area of tables and chairs that might have been called a plaza, though it was scarcely wider than a couple of alleys put side-by-side. After they finished up and rose to leave, they passed Gordon Hollenbeck and Gerald—they'd never learned his last name—who were headed into the Bizzy B. Gerald was an older man about Gordon's age, tall and thin, with a shiny bald head and a pencil-thin mustache. He had driven Gordon and the two of them up from the airport in his little red jalopy.

"Good to see you again," Gerald said, shaking their hands. "I see you've found the place to get a decent cup of joe. Gordon and I were thrilled when this place opened up. With my New York roots, I'm a bit of a coffee snob, and it can be hard to get decent coffee in the islands. Gordon tells me you're over in English Quarter?"

"Yeah," Boone said. "Not too far. Beautiful view—haven't checked out the interior yet. It's called *Hummingbird Haven*."

"Ah, Amber's rental cottage," Gordon said. "Splendid view."

"Where do you lads live?" Emily asked.

"*Lads* … oh I like this one. Makes me feel twenty years younger." Gordon pointed across The Road and up a rise. "Young lady, we have a little place behind the Saba Tourism office, up the hill a bit. The one with the red roof." He winked at her.

"Good one," she said.

"Well, we'll leave you two to enjoy your morning. I'm sure we'll bump into you again soon—that's the nature of Saba. Come on Gerald, it's croissant time!" And with that, the two gentlemen entered the bakery.

"Where to next?" Emily asked.

"Post office opens early. Let's see if anything made it yet, and then we can hit one of the grocery stores."

By mid-afternoon they had settled in and decided to swing back into town and see if Sid had found anything out about the potential break-in. Grabbing some soursop smoothies from Saba Snack, they went next door to the police annex, which actually shared the same storefront. Sid was sitting inside, somehow managing to look both bored and restless.

"Hey Sid," Boone said. "You don't look all that happy to be here."

"It's my ribs … can't get comfortable. Ah, you've found the smoothie shop next door, have you? You'll be Sabanized in no time. They have some of the best Wi-Fi, by the way. I'm actually on their network right now. Shhh … don't tell. Pull up a seat. I can pretend to book you, if that sounds like fun."

"Well, Emily did drop her coffee cup on the way over to our cottage." Boone said, folding his lanky form into a plastic chair.

"Hey!" Emily protested.

"Littering…" Sid tsked and shook his head solemnly. "Saba takes its ecotourism very seriously. She's nicknamed The Unspoiled Queen, and you, young lady, have spoiled her."

"Also, she snores."

Emily socked Boone in the biceps. "I do *not*! And I picked that coffee cup back up, after I accidentally dropped it while opening the lid to a rubbish bin."

"It *did* touch the ground, officer," Boone said solemnly. "Do you have handcuffs in the annex?"

"Absolutely."

"Okay fellas, I'm about ready to kick some serious bro butt. Maybe get Sophie to teach me a trick or two."

Boone looked at Emily, aghast. "Are you ... *threatening* Sid? An officer of the law?"

"Drink your soursop, string bean," Emily ordered. "So, Sid, the break-in ... *was* it a break-in?"

"The best answer I can give is 'maybe'. My father and I stopped by and the girl who was working Sunday says the hasp across the door wasn't broken when she locked up. But she said it had come loose a time or two before ... and she checked, and no money or inventory was taken."

"But..." Boone prompted.

"But I remembered you saying something about maps, so we called 'Crocodile' Johnson—he's pretty much the trail boss for the island. I asked him about any stash of maps other than the tourist ones and Croc said they kept some detailed survey maps at the shop, including some for unofficial trails that go back 400 years, as well as some partial maps of the old sulphur mine."

"Sulphur mine? I didn't know there was any mining on the island," Boone said.

"There isn't, not since the turn of the century, anyway. The mine is abandoned, and some of the tunnels are gated off. They haven't been fully explored. A few years ago, a tourist went missing—they found his mummified body a year later. It can get incredibly hot in there and the sulphur can make it difficult to breathe in places. Here, check it out." He pulled out his smart phone and scrolled through some photos before finding one and holding it up. In the shot, a sweaty Sid and Sophie were standing alongside a cave opening, smiles on their faces and yellow smears on their

T-shirts and shorts. "We took a tour. Really cramped in there! The mines are mostly sealed now with a single known entrance, but Croc thinks there are others."

"Hang on. I'm still working on the name *Croc*," Emily said. "There aren't crocodiles on Saba, are there?"

Sid smiled. "No. A big iguana or two, but no crocodiles. But if you met James—his real name is James—chopping through the brush of a trail with his cutlass, you'd see the name's pretty on-the-nose. I think he took it from that movie, *Crocodile Dundee*, but he's not Australian—eighth-generation Saban."

"So, were the maps there?" Boone asked.

"No. They were supposed to be in a stack in the back, but we couldn't find them."

"Why would anyone want to steal a bunch of old maps?" Boone mused.

"Maybe he's a cartography addict and needed a fix," Emily suggested.

Sid shook his head, thinking. "It seems like an unlikely thing to take. Boone, what you saw in the man's hand might have been his own map, just a tourist one. Saba Conservation's going to look around for the missing ones. Someone official might have borrowed them—maybe Ryan, who's the island's archaeological specialist. Heard he might be doing some excavations at the old abandoned village of Mary's Point."

"Makes sense," Boone said.

"Hey, here's something of interest. The boat we used to go after the submarine, that Viking, the *Wavy Davey*? The smuggler we impounded it from is in lockup at the station, but he's scheduled to be taken to Sint Maarten tomorrow. My father decided to have a final chat with him, and he's convinced that the man didn't act alone, that there was another man on board who must've been on island when we boarded the boat in Fort Bay."

"So, you think you've got a smuggler running around on the island?" Emily asked.

"Well, Saba has a long history of pirates and smugglers hiding out," Sid said. "The terrain is a natural fortress, and with there being no port here for so long, it was a good place for people on the run from the law."

"Will we never find a more wretched hive of scum and villainy?" Emily asked innocently.

"Nerd," Boone said, giving her a playful shove.

Sid laughed, getting the reference. "Some of the stories are greatly exaggerated, I'm sure, but I bet plenty of them are true. One of my favorites: they say privateers would bring captured ships here, and either repair, repaint, and rename them ... or strip them of parts and scuttle them in the deeper waters offshore. Kind of a maritime chop shop, I suppose."

"So, if there *was* a second smuggler," Boone said, "he'd have plenty of places to hide."

"Maybe, but chances are he's long gone. We're checking the passenger manifests for WinAir flights, and also the ferries to Saint Martin."

Boone looked at the old-fashioned clock on the back wall and rose from his chair. "We were thinking of grabbing an early dinner, if you'd care to join us. I'm supposed to be down at Scenery Scuba at seven a.m. and want to get a good night's sleep before my first day."

"I'm meeting Sophie later, but I'll join you another time. Know where you're going to eat?"

"Gordon said the pizza at Long Haul next door was great. And he's a New Yorker, so..."

"It *is* good, but they're closed Mondays. A lot of places stagger their days off. Try Bubba's above Sea Saba—they open at five-thirty."

"Thanks, we will," Boone said, as he held the door open for Emily.

"Good luck finding your smuggler," Emily sang as she bounced out the door into the late afternoon sunlight.

As the sun set, the man settled in to wait, the camp chair positioned perfectly in the shadows inside the skeleton of the unfinished cottage. Sitting well back from one of the windowless openings, he could just see the entrance to The Ladder, the steep stairs leading down from a cut in the low wall lining Ladder Road. A few days ago, he'd chatted up a group of young medical students at a bar in The Bottom. He'd ditched his workman's attire for a tight T-shirt and shorts, displaying his tanned physique to lure them in. He was a strikingly handsome man: his hair blond and sun-kissed, his shoulders broad and his body sculpted. Great strength and stamina were requirements for his calling.

He did not enjoy this part of his work—as far back as puberty he had found flirting excruciatingly awkward. Unsettling. It was like trying to speak a half-learned foreign language. Over time he had realized it was best to say little and let his good looks do most of the work. He had noted several prospects during that outing, but toward the end of the evening a valuable piece of information had tumbled forth from one drunken youth, leading him to adjust his plans. After all, selecting a candidate from a public gathering carried many risks. No, this new opportunity was ideal, and he suspected the fortuitous piece of trivia had been a gift from those he served.

The man had learned that the old customs house, an empty shell of a building halfway down The Ladder, was a popular make-out spot for young locals on the island. Moreover, the entrance to that spot was right across from his hideout. And to think, he'd almost remained at that other location, where no such opportunity would have presented itself, it being far too remote.

Those he served had provided him with what he needed, as they always did. All he'd have to do was wait … and watch. Anyone going down to the customs house after dark would definitely use the stairs and trail below. There was no guarantee he'd have any more luck tonight than he'd had last night, but he was confident his diligence would be rewarded in time.

Taking a long pull from a water bottle, the man relaxed and let his mind drift. It was only two short years ago that he had received his calling. A mission trip to Montserrat had sown the seeds: the awesome devastation that the Soufrière Hills volcano had wrought on the island's capital of Plymouth had filled him with an awe akin to a religious conversion. Nearly two decades before, a massive eruption had sent a pyroclastic flow roaring into the capital city of the tiny Caribbean island, burying the town in ash nearly five feet thick, killing numerous inhabitants and rendering the entire southern half of Montserrat uninhabitable. The volcanic material soon took on the consistency of concrete and now, like Pompeii, the town of Plymouth was entombed by nature itself. Witnessing the aftermath of such a profound *alteration* of what Man had built … it was as if the Earth itself was speaking to him. He had tried to explain it to one of the girls who

his window down. "You Boone Fischer?" came a voice with a lazy drawl. The voice belonged to a man in his forties, his skin tanned and sun-freckled, his hair bleached brown. His left arm, resting in the open window of the driver's side door, was sheathed in an elaborate tattoo sleeve.

"Yeah, I'm Boone. Are you Derrick Richardson?"

"That'd be me, but folks just call me 'Lucky'. And I'm guessin' this is your fellow submarine killer. Emily, right? Hold on one sec. Lemme park this sucker."

He pulled over to the side, close to where Sid had parked the day they'd taken the *Wavy Davey*. As Lucky came back over to them, Emily pointed up at the sign. "Saba Deep?"

"Oh, yeah, don't mind that. I haven't put a sign up yet. Saba Deep was an institution on this island, and I don't have the heart to take that down. They went out of business a few years back. Actually, their only boat had an accident…" He turned and pointed to the tiny harbor. "Sunk right over there, by that jetty."

"Well, we've had some recent experience with sinking ships…" Boone said.

"Not *mine*, ya better not! Only got one, at the moment. Shame about that smuggler boat you used. She was a beauty."

"Viking 48C," Boone said.

"Oh, you know boats?"

"Boone here was our dive op's go-to fixit man," Emily broke in. "But I'm the better skipper."

Lucky looked down at Emily with an appraising eye. "You two worked together back in Bonaire?" When they nodded, Lucky bit his lip in thought. "Well, here's the thing … we're new and operating at the margins, so I'm not really in a position to hire both of you."

"Oh, I'm just on vacation," Emily said quickly. "But if you happened to have a few free tanks lying around, I wouldn't mind hopping aboard as an extra diver anytime you're not full up. And I can offer my services at the wheel if you need an extra hand, yeah?"

"I dunno. How old are you?"

"Oh, come on, just 'cause I'm tiny ... I'm twenty-six." When Lucky raised an eyebrow at Boone, Emily plowed ahead. "Boone's twenty-nine, but he's got that old soul thing goin' on."

Boone smiled. "She's not pulling your leg, Lucky—this gal can drive a boat like nobody's business."

"You mind sharing your tips with her?"

"I dunno..." Boone hedged, feigning reluctance.

"He doesn't mind," Emily said, pushing past Boone to grab Lucky's hand in an ambush of a handshake. "Deal. Let me dive for free, and I'll help out and steal Boone's tips."

"She's also really good at dive briefings," Boone said.

Lucky chuckled. "Well, one thing at a time ... how about you two learn the dive sites before you start briefing. I'll go out with you today. Emily, you can tag along on the dives. We've only got a four-pack of divers at the moment so there'll be plenty of room. C'mon inside. We can chat while I open up."

"Hey, what's that wooden second-floor area, to the left there?" Emily asked as they started toward the door to the shop.

"Oh, that there used to be The Deep End. A bar and restaurant. Closed a few years ago. Actually, a big restaurant company in the States bought the whole building, both the restaurant and dive shop. But they weren't doing anything with it and I needed a place to start, so I negotiated a short-term lease. Figured they'd rather make *some* money than no money." He applied the key to the dive shop door and worked it aggressively until it finally turned. "Yeah … this place needs some work. I'm out on a lot of the dives to save money on staff, so I haven't had the time to get this place ship-shape. But with your friend helping out … maybe I can find myself an extra shore day here and there."

"How long you been on island?" Boone asked.

"Sold my house in Corpus Christi four months ago and moved here. My wife and I … well, guess it's ex now … we took a dive trip to Saba a few years ago and this place really spoke to me. After the divorce last year, she moved back home to California and I just didn't want to stay in the house a moment longer. So, one day I'm about to throw on this T-shirt with *I Survived the Saba Landing* on it—"

"Boone got me that shirt!" Emily broke in. "Oh, sorry … I interrupted your moment of epiphany, didn't I?" Emily bit her lower lip, looking sufficiently sheepish that a snort of laughter escaped Lucky's mouth.

"You, young lady, are a hoot. No apologies necessary. Anyhow, I took one look at that ratty old shirt and thought, 'Yeah, that's where I'm going.' I have a technical diver background from working oil platforms in the Gulf and figgered I could join a dive op, but when I heard Saba Deep left, I thought I'd open my own place."

"How long you been open?" Boone asked.

"Not long. Anders, the fella you switched with, was my first employee. You'll meet the others in a bit."

"So, are you and Sea Saba the only games in town?" Emily asked.

"There's another, Saba Diving. They've been around for almost twenty years. They got a nice 34-footer, *Big Blue*. I'm still just small potatoes." Lucky gestured to the two mesh bags beside the door. "Grab your gear and come on in. I'll give you the penny tour."

An hour later, Lucky led Boone and Emily around the little bay to the pier on the far side, passing a two-story building as they went. "That there is the Customs and Immigration Office. The passengers from the Saint Martin ferries come in through there so sometimes I hang out nearby, in case anyone's looking to dive but hasn't booked anything yet."

Boone nodded, remembering Sid saying they'd checked the passenger manifests for the ferries, looking for the arrested smuggler's partner—if, in fact, the individual existed. "How often do the ferries come and go?" he asked.

"There's two of 'em. The *Edge* and the *Dawn II* each come in three days a week." They turned the corner and started down the far pier. A sturdy slab of concrete over 200 feet long, the pier's surface was quite a bit higher than the decks of the dive boats moored alongside.

"Nice boats!" Emily said as they approached the nearest two— sleek forty-footers complete with flybridges.

"Yep, that they are. Wish they were mine. Those belong to Sea Saba. We're on the end."

He gestured toward a small center console dive boat at the end of the pier. With her white hull and red Bimini top, the boat looked like a nautical version of a Saba cottage. The name *Shoal 'Nuff* was along her bow in red letters.

"You bringing some fresh meat, Lucky?" called a voice from under the Bimini top. A shirtless young man, his body sculpted and deeply tanned, grabbed a support and swung up onto the gunwale. He tossed aside a lock of bleached-blond hair from his eyes, a cocky grin on his face. "Bonaire Boone finally showed up for wor—" He halted mid-sentence, his eyes taking in Emily. "Whoa ... bonus." His speech had the laid-back quality of a Cal-

high cliffs there. The 'fort' was actually some retaining walls holding back a bunch of boulders. When the pirates got into the gut, the Sabans knocked the supports loose and avalanches killed half the pirates and their leader. Irony there is, most of the Sabans dumping those rocks were likely descended from pirates themselves."

"They ever have rock slides?" Boone asked, looking up at the terrain directly above the port, where the cliffs were littered with scree and boulders.

"Don't say that too loudly, the island might hear you," Lucky quipped. "There've been a few rock slides on the western slopes, but nothing too major. Mount Scenery is a volcano, you know … so there might be some kinda seismic activity from time to time."

"I thought I read somewhere it was dormant," Boone said.

"Well, it's dormant until it isn't. There's some debate on this, but some are calling it 'potentially active.' There're some hot springs near where we're about to dive, for instance. Sensors picked up a burst of seismic events in 1992, but not much since then." He suddenly barked a laugh. "I just remembered … Will Johnson? He's our historian, lives up there on The Level above El Momo…" He pointed, and sure enough they were just passing below the cliffs that the El Momo cottages were set into. "Will was telling me about the time the University of the West Indies, down in Trinidad, called up Saba on the phone … saying 'Oh my God, are you all right?' They monitor seismic sensors in the Caribbean and they were acting like they thought Saba had been wiped out by an eruption."

"What happened?" Emily asked.

"Cow kicked the sensor," Lucky said, grinning. "Nah, the last full eruption was sometime before 1640. Actually, there's a whole *bunch* of these stratovolcanoes in the area. Fair number of the

Leeward Islands are built around one. You can see another one right over there."

Lucky pointed to the southeast. It was an exceptionally clear day and another island with a distinct cone on one end was in sight. Just beyond, another island was visible.

"I think our WinAir flight stopped there on our way over here. That's Statia, right?"

"Yep. Statia—Sint Eustatius if you wanna be wordy. The volcano there is called The Quill. And beyond that you can see Saint Kitts ... and it's not in sight, but Nevis is down there, just past Kitts. Both of them are centered on stratovolcanoes as well."

"You seem to know a lot about volcanoes," Emily said. "Are you a ... oh, what's the word ... you know, like Mr. Spock?"

Lucky laughed. "Vulcanologist? No. But for my oil rig diving work, I got a degree in geology. Just an area I'm interested in, is all."

They curved around the southeast corner of the island and started north. Boone found his eyes continuing to the east and he felt Emily's hand slip into his. He looked down at her, nodding.

"That's where that submarine was, wasn't it?" Lucky asked over the sound of the engine. "The one you two sank?"

"Well, we didn't exactly sink it," Boone said. "We rammed it, and then they pretty much took care of destroying it themselves. Broke the back of the boat we were on."

Just then, the boat gave a hitch and Boone felt a quick double shudder in his feet before everything returned to normal.

"Dammit," Lucky muttered.

"Feels like the transmission," Boone said.

"Yeah, probably. It happened last week but then didn't recur. I guess I was just hoping..."

"I can take a look at it when we reach the dive site," Boone suggested.

"Only two." Emily ascended the ladder, passing her lime green fins to Boone. "Actually, I spotted something I never saw in Bonaire. Bottom was eighty feet, some dark volcanic sand down there. There were three flying gurnards! One fanned out its pectoral fins like two peacock tails!"

A pair of fins sailed over the transom and Lucky came up the ladder, BC and tank in his free hand. "Chad's bringing up the rear. Current was starting to pick up toward the end. We were lucky to get in when we did. By afternoon, this woulda been no-go." He set his gear aside and returned to the stern, helping the remaining divers with their equipment as they came to the ladder.

"Hey, Lucky … what's that area up there with all the low grass?" Boone asked, pointing up to the cliff's edge before reaching down for a diver's fins. "I can see bits of a stone wall … some kind of mound of rocks."

"That's where the old sulphur mine is. There used to be a cable from up there to the Green Island rock, to shuttle down the sulphur. That mound is an old oven. You can't see the entrance of the actual mine from here, though. There's a cave opening down a little trail, to the left of the oven."

"Sid told us about the mine. Said it could be dangerous to go in there."

"I've been in once—hotter than hell and stinks to high heaven. Plenty cramped, too—had to crab walk in a couple places. Still a lot of sulphur in there. I slid along a wall and ended up with yellow streaks all over my clothes."

"So, people can go in there, then?"

"Yeah, you can hike down from Upper Hell's Gate, but they recommend you go with a guide and never go in alone."

"Huh. Guess someone didn't get the memo."

"See somebody up there? Probably someone with the conservation or archaeology groups. They've been looking for other entrances, but after a tourist died in there, all the side tunnels were gated and locked."

"Roll call," Chad called, grabbing a clipboard and reading off the names of their small group of divers. Even though a quick headcount had confirmed everyone was aboard, you always did a roll call.

Lucky jerked a thumb toward the cockpit. "Boone, we good to go?"

"Yeah, should be fine if you take it easy."

"All right. Release the mooring line, then come back here and tell me what you found. And Emily…" He gestured to the wheel. "Let's see what you can do."

Once they were underway, Lucky motioned Boone to join them. "So … thoughts on the engines?"

"You had a loose shaft coupling. One of the bolts was missing and a couple others were loose. I tightened those up with the torque wrench. I also found a small amount of fluid pooled in the bilge. Not a lot, but it was there. I couldn't pin anything down, though."

"All right. Well, that decides the next dive site. We'll do Tent Reef, just outside the bay. You'll go down with Anika and I'll stay up top—get my mechanic to come down in a couple hours. The grocery ship comes in tomorrow, and Fort Bay can get a little cramped—better to get it fixed today. Maybe that missing bolt's rattling around down there somewhere."

"She's handling fine right now," Emily said, gently turning the wheel to starboard as they made their way around the island.

"Don't jinx it, Em," Boone said.

"Not a chance. I have the magic touch," she replied breezily. "All boats know and love me."

Lucky laughed. "I'll take every good luck charm I can get. Keep at it. Once we reach Fort Bay, throttle down and I'll guide you to the mooring ball. I gotta have a word with Chad and our divers. Probably gonna need to cancel the afternoon dive."

While Lucky headed over to Chad, Boone leaned in toward Emily. "You better have some good footage of those flying gurnards."

"I got three great videos ... but maybe I'll keep them for myself. Until you do something to earn it."

Boone reached up between her braids and gave her a neck rub. "This do it?"

Emily was quiet for a few moments before mumbling something that Boone couldn't hear above the engines.

"What?"

"I said, 'That'll get you one video.' But knock it off, before I drive us into the rocks." She shouldered him. "So, what do you think? We going to like it here?"

Boone looked up at the towering island, its green flanks brilliant in the late-morning sun.

"I think we've found a quiet little corner of paradise."

7

The blond man tucked the detailed trail map into a pocket before grasping a thick root and pulling himself up along a steep section of the Middle Island Trail. In moments, he crested the slope and reached the dead end of Ladder Hill Road. Removing his sweat-soaked shirt, he mopped his face and glanced at a nearby cottage, its red roof and white walls peeking out of the dense shrubs at the base of a massive gumbo-limbo tree. The tree was impressive, its reddish bark curled up in places. The man's lip rose in a smirk as he remembered that locals on another island called it the "tourist tree," because it was red and peeling, like the sunburned vacationers who visited the Caribbean. Taking a few steps to the side, he peered between the leaves of an elephant ear plant. At the end of the obscured driveway was a small white car of some sort; many of the vehicles on this island were subcompacts of one kind or another. No sign of anyone. Not that he was concerned. This trail was one of the less-frequented ones and he hadn't seen a soul all morning.

He had set aside his utility coveralls, opting for typical hiking garb for his morning reconnoiter. The old cistern was right where the map said it would be, tucked into the side of the slope, partially obscured by overhanging foliage. Its stone-lined, rectangular shape looked a bit like a little swimming pool. Or a water-filled grave.

The man began walking back down the road to the unfinished house that he considered home base. The sun was approaching its zenith and his sculpted, sweat-soaked physique sparkled. He took great pride in keeping himself in peak physical condition. Yes, there was vanity in it, he knew … but the end result served a greater design. Most of those he selected were not keen to fulfill their purpose, but his phenomenal strength made their reticence irrelevant.

Halfway to his hideout, a sharp ding sounded from a pocket of his shorts. Extracting a cheap burner phone he'd procured, he noted that he had a message. The cell signals were surprisingly good on much of the island, but the trail he'd just been on was fairly remote from most of the villages. He started to put the phone back in his pocket, but it rang in his hand. The man sighed and answered the call. There was only one person who had this phone's number.

"Yes?"

"I called you an hour ago—vere have you been?" came a heavily accented voice, its tone brimming with irritation.

"Busy."

"Listen, I can't get a signal in there so every time I call you I have to crawl out of *das verdammte Höllenloch*. If I call, I expect you to answer!"

"Sorry. I lost my signal as well. I just now got your message. Shall I listen to it?"

"*Nein*, ve are talking now! I need more water."

The blond man did not respond, lifting his gaze up to the cloud-wreathed peak of Mount Scenery and enjoying a cooling breeze that chose that moment to kick up.

"Did you hear me? *Hallo? Gott im Himmel*, did I lose you? I said I need more—"

"I just brought you water. And food. And blankets. And extra batteries. And the map you asked for. We had an agreement. I wasn't to visit you again until I have your passport."

"Do you have any idea how hot it gets in here? I'm going through the water faster than I expected."

"It was your choice to hide out in there."

"It vas the *best* choice! I have no idea if my partner talked and if he did, the authorities vill be looking for me. Ve have hidden things here before and I know much of the layout. But I confess, I don't remember it *smelling* so much; it stinks like rotten eggs in here! And I *know* it's hotter than the last time ve used it. I need more water. If you vant your money, you'll haf to bring it."

The blond man was silent again for a moment. The trek to make these deliveries was not an easy one, particularly with a case of water bottles, and he risked exposure himself.

"Very well. Another thousand."

"Anoth—" The other side of the conversation descended into a muffled torrent of Teutonic obscenities. "Ach.... agreed! Vhatever it takes to get out of *dieser verflucht* place."

"I will bring more in a few days then. And you will need to show me the money at that time—*before* I return with your new passport."

"Vhat, you don't trust me?"

"Of course not. You're a smuggler. And from what I overheard around the island, when your boat was blown up a bag of money went down with it."

"That vas Santiago's share. He foolishly left it in the hidden compartment vhen ve vent into town for supplies. I haf my cut—and you vill haf yours vhen you deliver my papers. That is, assuming I'm not dead of dehydration. Believe me vhen I say this: You vill *never* find me in here unless I vant you to. Haf you met vith the forger yet?"

"No, he's off island. He'll be back day after tomorrow and I'm meeting with him in the afternoon."

"*Es ist gut.* I vill call you after."

"Call me before six," the blond man said. "I have work to do in the evenings."

He ended the call and resumed his walk, halting suddenly as the unfinished cottage came into view. There was a man there. Skinny, in his late fifties, dressed for hiking: a walking stick in hand, a slouch hat atop his head, and a pair of binoculars around his neck. The hiker examined the SUV and the buckets next to it, then walked to the side of the cottage and peered into the interior through the skeletal walls. After a moment, he stepped back, looking around the grounds.

The blond man casually resumed walking, calling out with a wave as he neared the hiker. "Good day for it, huh?"

The hiker looked startled. "Oh! Hello. Yes indeed, beautiful day."

The blond man advanced. "Looks like someone's building a house."

"Yes," the hiker said absently. "It seems that someone is doing some work on it. It's just that I knew the owner. American fellow. Died last month. Odd. Ah well, I'll give his niece a call. Maybe they sold the property." He turned and offered his hand. "I'm Chris. Chris Brady."

The blond man smiled and took his hand, giving it a shake. "William."

"My goodness, you've got a grip." He nodded at the blond man's shirtless body. "You a weightlifter or something?"

"William" laughed somewhat awkwardly. "Not really. I just go to a gym and try to eat right."

"You from the States?" Chris asked.

"Yes, just a tourist, sad to say. Your island is beautiful."

"Well, on behalf of the island, thank you." He pulled a hand-kerchief from a pocket and mopped his forehead under the brim of his hat. "I must say, I don't see many hikers up this way. If you were looking for The Ladder, it's actually over there." He indi-cated the break in the wall down the road.

"Oh, no, I was hiking the Middle Island Trail. Wanted to check out Well's Bay."

"Really! I'm actually headed there myself. I'm a bit of a birder, you see." He tapped the binoculars.

The man who was not William thought quickly about the sights he'd seen on his trek. "Hey, what's that white bird with a red beak ... long, thin tendril of a tail...?"

Chris's face lit up. "The Red-billed Tropicbird! That's what I'm looking for! They nest in the rocky cliffs and I heard some were around. Where did you see them?"

"I'll show you."

"No, don't be silly! You just came from there."

"It's no trouble, I love to hike. It's why I came here. Besides, this way I'll be hiking in the other direction. A whole new per-spective. I know just where those birds are."

"Very well. Thank you, William. Lead on."

The man who was not William pulled his shirt back on and led the way.

❖ • ❖

"Look there!" Chris hissed excitedly, pointing to a tree limb on the slope above them. "An American Kestrel!"

"William" looked up and spotted the tiny brown bird. It looked like a miniature hawk.

Chris's binoculars were up and locked onto the bird in an instant. "It's one of the smallest birds-of-prey in the world." He chuckled. "You know, locally it's called the "Killy Killy," because of the sound it makes.

The blond man made no response, continuing to stare at the deadly little bird. He glanced at the man beside him, noting a band of lighter skin on the ring finger of the left hand that held the binoculars. "You married?"

"Hmm? Oh, no, not anymore. Wife couldn't take the isolation here. Divorced. I live alone, but I don't mind the quiet. You? Big strapping man like you, I imagine you'd have your pick of the girls."

"William" felt his jaw involuntarily clench before he forced it to relax once more, his face remaining impassive. "No. Just haven't found the right woman." Then he turned and continued down the trail. They were now over a quarter mile from Ladder Road. He angled off the trail on the seaward side, stepping onto an outcrop overlooking a rocky ravine that dropped down toward the sea.

"Where are you going? Is this where you saw the Tropicbirds? Down in that gut?" Chris pushed through the dense foliage that ringed the little outcrop.

"Yes. Right down there." The man pointed before stepping back to allow the birdwatcher to pass him.

Chris carefully moved nearer the edge, lifting his binoculars with excitement. "Thank you so much ... I've only seen them a few times." He searched. "I ... I don't see them...."

"Why did you have to know the owner?"

The birder lowered his binoculars and turned back to the blond man. "I'm sorry ... what?"

"Killy killy."

Chris Brady's eyes registered a flash of realization as the man's powerful arms shot forward with blinding speed, grabbing the birder's head in a vice-grip and twisting savagely. A grisly crunch sounded, punctuated by a muted *pop*. The man who was not William then grabbed his prey by the belt buckle and shirt collar, lifting him completely over his head and hurling him down into the dense underbrush a hundred feet below the outcrop. Leaves rustled and branches snapped for several seconds as the lifeless body crashed down through the foliage, quickly becoming lost from sight.

What an inconvenience. He stepped forward and looked down, searching for any sign of the fallen birder. Assessing the kill, he felt quite proud of how he'd handled it. A tragic fall, that was all, such a shame. And it would likely be some time before the body was discovered. The act itself had aroused nothing inside him, but this was not a surprise to the blond man. He didn't swing that way. And even then, he preferred to use his instrument. No, this had required a simpler method. It had been an obstacle placed in his path and he had overcome it, nothing more.

Glancing down, the man picked up the fallen walking stick. It was constructed of polished wood with a little leather loop to thread onto the wrist, and atop its head was a tiny compass. He dug that out and pocketed the trophy, before tossing the stick down to join its owner.

As he turned to go back to the trail, a flash of white caught his eye. A beautiful seabird with a bright red beak and flowing tail glided by the nearby cliffs, heading out to sea.

"Smart man," Boone said, dropping down to the deck behind Emily, having helped the last of the divers to the pier. "Piss her off, she'll bite your kneecaps—*oof!*"

Em cut him off with a swift elbow to the bread basket. "No size jokes from you, beanpole."

"Hey, Chad!" Lucky called out.

Up on the pier, where he was flirting with one of the Wisconsin divers, the tanned Californian turned back to the boat. "Yeah, boss?"

"Go tell Anika we're done for today. And ask her to call Lucius, let him know we're back." Lucky turned back to Boone and Emily. "You two can take off. My guy will be here shortly. I'll see you bright and early tomorrow."

"Here, gimme that whiteboard," Boone said. "I'll jot down a few things he should check."

While Boone scribbled some notes, Emily grabbed her gear and hopped up to the pier to head to the shop. As she did so, her eyes drifted to the right. Past a little snack shop called Pop's Place and a shower/bathroom facility was a long, blue mural. Emily strolled over to it, her sandals slapping on the pavement. The mural was beautiful, depicting underwater scenes teeming with fish and corals. The phrase *Welcome to Saba, Captain Leo Chance Pier* was written across the top, but another set of words caught her eye: *SYMBIOSIS* and *Nothing in this universe exists alone.* From these words, a watery wave flowed, with additional phrases woven into the fabric of the painted current: *Every drop of water, every human being, all creatures in the web of life, and all ideas in the web of knowledge are part of an immense, evolving, dynamic whole as old, and as young, as the universe itself.* Em reached out and placed her palm on the painted surface, warmed by the tropical sun. *Nothing in this universe exists alone.*

"It's beautiful, isn't it?"

Em turned and saw Sophie approaching, Boone at her side. She couldn't help but notice Sophie's hand resting on Boone's forearm as he gripped his gear bag. "Um … yes, beautiful," Emily said. "Both the painting *and* the poetry."

"Hang on," Boone said, breaking loose from Sophie and moving to a green portion of the mural, the depiction of a Saban hillside punctuated with a cottage and three portraits of prominent Sabans. One of them was a woman, her name displayed beneath her face. "Rebecca Levenstone. Is this…?"

"That's my great-grandmother. I *told* you she was a legend."

"What are you doing down here?" Emily asked. "Don't you have fire brigade work at the airport?"

Sophie smiled and waved an elegant hand in casual dismissal. "Lunch break. Next plane isn't for a few hours and I figured I'd catch you two when you came up for air. I asked Anika to give me a call when your second dive was finishing up. Sid's taking a break too and he's firing up the grill. Can I tempt you with lunch? We've got shrimp skewers and some fresh yellowtail snapper."

"Sounds great," Boone said. "Em?"

"Sure," Em said, smiling broadly beneath her sunglasses. "Shrimp and snapper sounds scrummy."

After a delicious meal, the four sat in plastic patio furniture in the tiny backyard of Sophie's cottage.

"Tasty grub, Sid," Emily said. "What's for afters?"

"Afters?" Sid asked.

"She means dessert," Boone said.

"Got a sweet tooth, do you?" Sophie teased. "Sid, why don't you run Emily down to the Bottom Bean to grab some dessert for us ... and get me some of those cookies I like."

"Oh, no, that's okay. I was just teasing," Emily protested.

"Nonsense! It's right down the street. Sid can show you some of the shops on the way and Boone can stay here and keep me company. Maybe tell me a little about capoeira. I confess, I've always been curious about that martial art. It seems so ... flamboyant. Not brutally practical like Krav Maga."

"Oh ... okay," Emily said. "Boone, you want anything special?"

"No, I'm good."

"You sure? They might have something with key lime in it, I know how you love it."

Boone smiled and set aside his bottle of water, starting to get up. "I'll come along if you want."

"No, don't be silly, you two can talk karate chops and Sid here can tell me what it's like being an island cop!" Emily grabbed Sid's arm and dragged him around the corner of the cottage toward the road.

"Easy," Sid said, wincing. "Ribs are still healing."

After they left, Sophie sipped at an orange soda, smiling at Boone until he broke the silence. "You really want to talk martial arts?"

"We could. But in show-and-tell, the best part is always ... 'show'. So ... show me."

Boone shrugged, unfolded his long limbs from the lawn chair, and rose to his feet. Setting the patio furniture off to the side, he cleared a section of tropical grass and kicked off his sandals. Sophie drained her soda and moved her chair, shedding her shoes as well.

Boone noted her bare feet. "You looking to spar?"

"Maybe in a moment. I want to watch you first."

"Fair enough. Before I start, show me your stance."

"For Krav?" Sophie shrugged and barely moved, continuing to stand in nearly the same manner, though Boone spied a slight widening of her feet and a barely noticeable dropping of her center of gravity.

"Subtle," Boone noted. "But at its core, your stance is similar to most of the hard-form martial arts, starting from a strong, stable platform. Capoeira is about fluidity of motion and unpredictability." He began a *ginga* step, shifting his weight as he stepped back and to the side, swinging alternate arms up in a horizontal block, then repeating the process in the other direction in a continuous flow of motion. "Capoeira was developed by slaves in Brazil, back when it was controlled by Portugal. The slaves adapted an ancient fighting style from Angola in Africa, incorporating dance and acrobatics to hide its true intent from slave-owners. At least, that's the narrative ... But it was pretty clear to the authorities it was an effective fighting style. The Portuguese used to arrest its practitioners."

"So ... your stance isn't stationary?" Sophie asked, intrigued. She circled around him, watching intently.

Boone effortlessly shifted his orientation, tracking her. "This is called the *ginga*. This is the base movement and lets a *capoeirista* hide his or her intentions, rapidly flowing from attack to defense. And where you might block an attack, the *capoeirista* will generally try to evade and counterattack."

"It doesn't seem rooted..." Sophie said, before suddenly taking an aggressive step toward Boone.

Boone quickly executed a cartwheel, an *aú*, tumbling rapidly around her flank and dropping into a *negativa* crouch. The instant he planted he snapped a quick *martelo de negativa* kick, stopping his instep just shy of Sophie's knee.

Sophie let out an appreciative hiss of breath. "That would have been it for my knee. And you did that from the ground—most styles, you want to stay off your back."

"When I incorporate Brazilian Jiu-jitsu into the mix, I'm quite comfortable fighting down here."

Sophie smiled and offered a hand to Boone. He gave her a sidelong look but allowed her to help him up. The instant he was standing she executed a quick wrist-locking maneuver that had him slapping her thigh, tapping out in surrender. She let him go, her eyes sparkling over a broad smile.

Boone shook his head. "I *knew* you were going to do that, and you still … you are *fast*, Sophie!"

"In Krav Maga, the quicker the fight's over, the better. But I didn't mean to steal your thunder. Show me something special."

"Okay," said Boone, grinning as he looked around the yard. He grabbed his half-full water bottle and strolled to a bamboo tiki torch, lifting the metal cap to peer inside. The wick was dry, the reservoir empty.

"You've probably noticed, we don't have many mosquitos on Saba," Sophie remarked. "We haven't filled that in ages."

"Perfect." Boone set the bottle into the reservoir and backed away.

"Don't break my torch," Sophie admonished.

Boone smiled and started a *ginga*, incorporating a few tumbles and cartwheels, maintaining his orientation on the tiki torch.

"That's all very pretty," Sophie said. "But—"

Boone spun his entire body into a compass half-moon kick, one of the fastest and most impressive moves in his arsenal. His heel struck the bottle with tremendous force, sending it flying against the roof of the cottage, where it ricocheted back in an arc. Boone caught the dented bottle in mid-air, uncapping it and chugging the remaining water.

Sophie stood, mouth agape. "No fucking way."

Boone grinned ear to ear. "Actually, I meant to send it *over* the roof. Happy accident, though. I was still thirsty."

"What ... what *was* that?"

Boone popped the lid back onto the tiki torch. "It's called *meia lua de compasso*, the "King of Kicks" in capoeira. It shows up as a finisher move in mixed martial arts matches from time to time."

"I admit, with all that bouncing around, I didn't think you'd be that accurate."

Boone shrugged. "Stationary target. In a real fight there's a good chance it will miss, but it almost always forces the opponent back, creating some distance. And if my opponent retreats, I can continue the rotation and throw another." He tossed the bottle into an orange recycling bin at the rear of the cottage. "Okay Sophie, now it's your turn to show. Whattaya got for me?"

Over the next few minutes, the two demonstrated some of their favorite techniques, slowly transitioning into some light sparring. Finally, Sophie stepped back.

"How would you take me down?"

Boone looked at the grassy ground. "Here? With no mat?"

"It's fairly soft. I train out here all the time. Come on. Take me down. If you can."

Boone had been watching Sophie closely. Clearly formidable, she was capable of dishing out some serious hurt, and she also exhibited discipline, not given to wild, uncontrolled moves. It wasn't often he got to spar with someone his match, so he began a *ginga* step. This time it was a little less showy and deceptively casual. Sophie squared off in a solid stance, arms held up defensively, her eyes locked on Boone's. He let his *ginga* drift closer to her and thought about an attack. The thought reached his eyes and Sophie saw it, striking out toward his glottal notch, the hollow at the base of his throat.

But Boone's thought was only that, a surface aggression and not his true intention. When she lashed out, he fell back and to the side, planting his hands and kicking his long legs into a *tesoura*, scissoring one leg against her hips at the front while the other leg swept her legs from behind, sending her to the ground on her back. Transitioning to jiu-jitsu, he scrambled to immobilize her in a controlled joint lock, but she had the same idea and he felt pressure on his wrist and elbow. In an instant, they were twined together in a tangle of arms and legs, both tapping out their surrender in fits of laughter.

"Thought you had me, didn't you?" Sophie breathed in his ear.

"Seems like your *chat* is going well," came a familiar voice.

Boone looked up to find Emily at the edge of the cottage, a little paper bag of pastries dangling from her fingers. He quickly untangled himself and stood. "Just a little sparring," he said, a bit out of breath.

"Uh-huh."

"Where's Sid?" Sophie asked, still on the grass.

"We stopped by the police station on the way back. His dad had to talk to him, so I came back by my lonesome." She smacked the paper bag against her bare leg a few times, her huge sunglasses hiding her eyes. "So ... which one of you was winning? It was hard to tell."

"Em..."

She swung her wrist up, tossing him the bag. "Guess what, you're in luck. They actually had key lime cookies. I already ate mine." She abruptly pivoted and headed around the side of the cottage.

Boone pocketed the little bag and slipped on his sandals. "Sophie, thanks for the lunch. I better…"

"Yes, you better…" she said, looking a bit embarrassed. "I was going to drop you two off in Windwardside on the way back to the airport, but…"

"Yeah … not a good idea. We'll walk a bit. Grab a cab." He trotted toward the street. Emily was half a block away, walking briskly toward town. Boone quickened his pace a little, catching up with her after a couple of minutes. He fell into stride with her, walking in silence for a while.

"Em … I know it's a clichéd line," he finally said. "But in this case, it really does apply. Nothing happened."

"I know."

They walked a bit further. This time Emily broke the silence, stopping abruptly beneath the brilliant red boughs of a flamboyant tree. "I know nothing happened. But I also know what it *looked* like."

Boone started to speak, but clamped his mouth shut when Emily raised a finger at him. She removed her sunglasses, tucking them into the neck of her T-shirt.

"I came here for you, Boone. I left my life in Bonaire to come here *with you*."

Her green eyes took on a shimmer and once again Boone began to say something, but Emily reached up and pinched his lips shut.

"Hang on a tick. I've got a point I'm trying to make and I'm going to get there." She released her lip grip. "You're a very intuitive man, Boone," she said, her green eyes flashing up at him. "You can sense things … I don't even know *how* you do it sometimes. So, you *had* to know I'm having a few fits of jealousy around Sophie. It may not be rational, but it doesn't have to *be* rational. I know nothing happened, I know you two were just sparring, but if you even for a second thought that seeing you rolling around on the ground with her might make me feel a lump in my throat, then you shouldn't have done it."

Boone felt a throat lump of his own as he gazed down at her. Above, the leaves and flowers of the flamboyant tree whispered in the tropical breeze. After a moment he nodded. "You're right. I'm sorry."

Emily watched him for several seconds before the ghost of a smile appeared on her lips. "I think you are. Okay then." She popped her sunglasses back on her face and grabbed his hand, pulling him back into a leisurely stroll. "You try your cookie? They're pretty good."

9

The next morning, as Boone and Emily reached the dive shop, they found Fort Bay bustling, numerous cars and trucks already parked, awaiting the week's delivery of goods from Saint Martin. Two-thirds of the main pier was taken up by a large green-and-yellow cargo ship, the *Mutty's Pride*. Sea Saba's two forty-footers, *Sea Dragon* and *Giant Stride*, were moored ahead of the *Mutty's* bow and the *Shoal 'Nuff* was right where they'd left it, on the smaller Fisherman's Pier.

"Grocery Day is de only day fresh food comes in," their taxi driver said, an eighth-generation Saban known locally as Steady Peddy. He waved at a group of people standing near the Customs and Immigration office. "A lot of de restaurants and hotels send someone down, hoping to get de best produce and meats."

Boone thanked Peddy and paid him. At some point he'd need to rent a car, but there seemed to be a particular art to driving on Saba and he didn't feel confident enough to try his hand at it yet.

Lucky came out of the dive shop to greet them. "Hey, Boone, I want to thank you again for your help with the engine. Got'er patched up and should be good to go."

"Glad to hear it. You our captain again today?"

"Nope. Anika's gonna run the show this morning." He pointed toward the dive boat and Anika, wearing a broad-brimmed Panama hat, gave them an enthusiastic wave. "She was pretty insistent. Just as well, I've got a lot of things to catch up on and I need to keep an eye on Tropical Storm Irma. See where she's headed. Set up a few contingency plans."

Boone hadn't had a lot of experience with major storms during his years as a dive instructor on Curaçao and Bonaire, the ABC Islands being outside the Hurricane Belt. In his entire time in those islands, only Hurricane Matthew had come close, and the damage in Bonaire had been negligible. Even his time at the University of Miami had been quiet. "Is there any cause for concern?" he asked.

"Still early days. It's not yet a hurricane and several models have it curving up and out. For now, get diving!"

"Permission to board, Captain?" Boone called out, as he and Emily brought their gear to the boat.

"Permission granted," Anika replied with a demure smile.

They hopped aboard, joining Anika in the cockpit, where she was clearing the whiteboard of Boone's repair notes and the last dive's artwork and dive plan. "What's the plan today?"

"We've got the group of four from Wisconsin again today. Sea is still calm, so you're in for a treat. We're going up to Third Encounter."

"Ooh, I read about that," Emily said. "That's that huge off-shore pinnacle, yeah?"

"Yes. Eye of the Needle, they call it."

"Looking forward to it," Boone said.

Anika bit her lip in excitement. "I promise you, this will be different from anything you dived in Curaçao or Bonaire." She shook her head, a shy smile on her face. "I still can't believe you're here, the very one who taught me to dive. It's so small, this world of ours."

"And now, *you* get to teach me. Looking forward to following your lead. Assuming I'm not stuck on the boat, fixing something."

"Oh, you'll be down there with me. Both of you. Chad can stay up top. Speaking of which, where is he? Excuse me." She pushed past Boone, giving his arm a little squeeze as she did so.

Boone quickly glanced at Emily.

One eyebrow arched up from behind her sunglasses, but she didn't look at him as she adjusted her gear. A smile grew on her face. "You're wondering if I'm jealous of her."

Boone shook his head slowly. "You're *not.*"

"Good boy. Glad to see your intuition is back. No, you look at Anika like she's a student and she looks at you as a mentor. Sophie ... well ... she looked at you *quite* differently."

"You guys talking about Sophie?" Chad set a yellow Igloo cooler down on the pier and hopped into the boat. "Man, she is *smoking!* What I wouldn't give to—"

"Oh, hey Sid!" Emily suddenly exclaimed in a loud, cheery voice.

Chad went white and whirled around to discover Anika crossing the street.

"Oh, my mistake," Emily said, dripping innocence. "It's Anika. Silly me."

Boone stifled a laugh as Chad shook his head and grabbed the Igloo, stowing it in a corner of the cockpit.

"The divers just pulled up," Anika said as she reached the boat. "We'll get an early start."

After rounding the coast of Saba and heading north for several minutes, Anika cut the wheel to port and started heading out to sea.

"The Third Encounter dive site is part of a group of sea mounts," Anika said, over the roar of the engines. "There's also Twilight Zone, Outer Limits, and Mount Michel. The big pinnacle at Third Encounter is called Eye of the Needle. It thrusts up from the ocean floor to within ninety feet of the surface. This is going to be a deep dive, so help me watch our divers. Short bottom time, no one below 110 feet. With the steep drop-off and the open ocean alongside, there's a decent chance of seeing some bigger pelagics. Caribbean reef sharks, hawksbill turtles. If we're really lucky, maybe a manta ray. Sea Saba actually saw humpbacks out here a few years ago."

"Tell me about the sharks," Boone said. Like many divers, he had a fascination with the sleek predators. Bonaire was not known for sharks, and in his time there Boone could count the number of times he'd seen them on his fingers and toes. Not counting nurse sharks, of course. Those docile bottom-feeders were a common sight in most islands.

"Saba is known for its reefies, the Caribbean reef sharks," Anika said. "Some dives you'll see five or six, and some of them can get pretty big. And we've got a lot of nurse, too, of course."

"Any other kinds?"

"Personally, I haven't seen any other types, but I've heard we get the occasional hammerhead or blacktip at the deeper sites. And way out that way—" she gestured to the southwest "—the Saba Bank is a huge, protected area. A few fishermen are allowed to go there. There, you might see tigers, bulls, silkies. But here, you'll see mostly reefies."

"Man, don't turn your back on a reefy," Chad said, joining them at the wheel as he grabbed a cup of water. "They've been getting aggressive."

"No, they haven't," Anika said with annoyance. "You just pick the wrong times to spear lionfish. Are there a bunch of reefies around? Wrong time."

The gossamer-finned lionfish was very beautiful, but it was an invasive species with venomous spines and a voracious appetite. Once nonexistent in the Caribbean, they were now everywhere. "Do the dive ops organize culls?" Boone asked.

"Sometimes," Chad said. "But I always carry my spear and tube on the boat. Several restaurants pay good money for them."

"Well, no lionfish hunting today," Anika said. "My boat, my rules. We're coming up on the mooring buoy. Once Chad ties us off, watch me draw up the dive plan and then I'll do the briefing.

◆ ◆ ◆

Ten minutes later, seven divers slipped beneath the waves. Having three divemasters guiding four divers would normally be considered overkill, but in this case Boone and Emily were largely along for the ride, learning the site as they kept an eye on their Wisconsin quartet. The dive began very differently from a typical Bonaire dive: they followed the mooring line down to a low plateau and then left it, swimming into a wall of empty blue water, the bottom vanishing completely. Boone noted Anika checking a compass from time to time. He took a moment to look at each of the recreational divers—everyone seemed calm and focused on Anika. He glanced over at Emily, her distinctive green and gray wetsuit and lime green fins making her easy to spot. At this depth, the greens had begun to wash out, but her fins were still the brightest of the bunch. He flashed a quick OK sign, and she returned it, then opened her eyes wide, sweeping her arms out in an expansive gesture. Boone took this to mean *Look at all this open ocean!* He nodded back and flashed another OK sign as an affirmative.

Diving back in the ABC islands meant largely hugging the reefs, with the occasional wreck dive. Here, swimming blindly into the blue was equal parts exhilarating and disorienting, with nothing but water on every side and the abyss below. But then, out of the blue ahead, a dark shape began to form. A school of horse-eye jacks floated nearby, their silver flanks flashing. As the divers drew nearer, the shape's features sharpened and the Eye of the Needle was revealed. Nearing it, more and more fish appeared, some in the blue waters surrounding it, others swimming in and out of the nooks and crannies of the coral, all of them drawn to this upthrust focal point in the middle of the sea.

At this depth, colors became muted, but even so, Boone could tell the pinnacle was completely armored in colorful corals. Anika began a gentle circle around the pinnacle and the Wisconsin divers followed, Boone and Emily bringing up the rear. The group made several circuits of the Eye, and Boone was happy to see no one pushing the depth limit. As he reached the far side on the third time around, he felt a tap on his arm. Emily. She placed her flattened hand vertically on her head, like a dorsal fin. *Shark.* She pointed. About twenty feet below them, out in the blue, a grayish-brown shark swam gracefully toward the pinnacle. It was hard to precisely gauge size underwater, but Boone guessed it had to be nearly seven feet in length. After a moment it turned and headed back into the blue, where it faded from view. Then another appeared, the same species, but smaller than the first. Boone was just pointing it out to Emily when two loud clangs sounded. A tank banger. Boone looked to the front of the group, noting other heads swiveling to and fro. Sound travels much faster through liquid than through air, and the human brain has trouble determining the direction of sounds underwater. In this case, the context soon made it clear where to look. It was a deep dive and their bottom time was nearly up. Sure enough, it was Anika. Up ahead, she was signaling the divers with a hand gesture that it was time to swim back to the mooring line.

———◆·◆———

Back aboard the *Shoal 'Nuff*, the Wisconsinites excitedly discussed the dive while Boone freed the boat from the mooring. Emily joined Anika in the cockpit and the young Dutch girl offered her the wheel.

"Lucky said you're quite the skipper and I should let you drive a bit."

"Lucky's a wise man. Where to?"

Anika pointed toward the slopes on Saba's western flank. "You see that gray area? That's a spot that had a landslide. We're going to the left of it."

Emily throttled up, bringing the little boat just above cruising speed. "Everything's so close here!"

Boone joined them. "What's that little building there?" he asked. A small white building sat atop a sheer cliff and as they drew closer, they could see what looked like zig-zagging walls leading up to it, rising almost vertically from the sea.

"I'm telling you, it's a nautilus!" one of them said, a blond woman in her late twenties. "I watched a nature show about them. They're kind of like a squid with a shell on its back."

The other diver seemed skeptical. "I dunno, Amy," he said. "Nautiluses are only in the Pacific."

"Yeah?" said Chad, sidling up to them and tossing a lock of hair aside as he gave Amy a grin. "That's what they said about lionfish … and look at them now! Naw, this lovely lady is right—that's a nautilus shell. That's why I brought you over to it. Pretty cool, huh? Musta gotten out of an aquarium or something."

Boone thought that highly unlikely. The nautilus, an ancient cousin of the squid and octopus, had never been seen outside of the Indian and Pacific oceans. He caught Anika snickering under her bandana and sidled over to her, grabbing Emily by the arm as he passed. "What?" he whispered.

She leaned into them. "That 'nautilus' he thinks he discovered is the reason he always wants to do that dive, so he can show off to the divers. That shell is a lawn ornament someone put down there. Chad still hasn't figured it out."

"Oh, that is rich … and you let him go on about it?" Emily said.

"I always catch the divers later and tell them … and then beg them not to tell *him*."

"You cheeky imp," Emily said, clearly impressed. "It's always the shy ones, hiding under bandanas. We're gonna need to go for drinks."

"I'd like that," Anika said.

"Am I invited?" Boone asked.

"Nope!" Emily chirped. "You can take Chad out for a beer while Anika and I have sophisticated tropical drinks, and she tells me all about what you were like back in Curaçao."

Anika laughed. "Maybe Martini Night at Scout's? They have karaoke."

"Karaoke! Oh, Booooone … guess what, *now* you're invited."

"Kill me now."

Just then, a Saba Police car came down the hill and passed by the dive boat, its white body adorned with orange and blue stripes. It pulled up near the Customs and Immigration office and a burly man with a mustache got out of the driver's seat while Sid got out of the passenger side. Boone exited the boat and headed toward them. In the rear of the vehicle he could see the shape of a man.

"Hey, Boone!" Sid called out. "Come meet my father."

The mustachioed man advanced to greet Boone, extending a meaty hand. "Boone Fischer, I'm Captain Clark Every. Dutch Caribbean Police." He had a slight Saban accent, but not nearly as strong as some Boone had heard on the island. "I want to thank you for keeping my boy safe the other day. He was pretty banged up after the explosion, and you got him safely off that smuggler's boat. Speaking of which…" He motioned Boone over to the car. Clark reached in to the driver's door and lowered the rear windows. The man in back looked up at them. "Say hello to Santiago Velasquez. At least that's what his papers say his name is. We caught him trying to get back aboard the *Wavy Davey*. Santi, this is the man who crashed your pretty boat into a submarine."

"Actually, that was Emily who did the ramming," Boone corrected.

The man looked at them sullenly, then back down at his shoes.

"We're pretty sure he had an accomplice, but Santi isn't talking, and I can't hold him any longer. As soon as the grocery ship heads out and the Edge ferry docks, I'm taking him over to Sint

Maarten." Clark gave the island name a little touch of Dutch, indicating the Dutch half of Saint Martin, as opposed to the French portion. "Sid, I need to talk to Immigration. Make yourself comfortable. Mr. Fischer … a pleasure."

As his father strode away, Sid joined Boone on the left side of the car. "Where's Emily?"

"She's still on the dive boat with Anika."

"Hey, Sophie told me about the sparring and the, um … aftermath."

Boone waved it off. "Water under the bridge. I think. But tell her I'm on a sparring sabbatical. And Sid, I'm sorry if—"

"Oh, no worries. Sophie's been dying for a good sparring partner. She's tried to train *me* but it's just not my thing. Honestly, I'm happy to let someone else get beaten up for a change."

"Hey, I'm thirsty." The prisoner, looking up at them, appeared tired.

Sid sighed and turned to Boone. "Keep an eye on him, would you? I'll grab some water bottles from Pop's." With that, he trotted across the road.

As soon as he was across, the prisoner spoke in a low voice. "You sink the boat, uh?"

"Yeah. Explosion broke her back."

"She was a beautiful boat."

Boone nodded, not saying anything.

"You find the money?"

"We did. It was in a hidden compartment in the flybridge."

Santiago nodded. "It sink too, yes?"

"Probably. The navy said they didn't find it. The bag was full of money and gear. We took a couple of the guns out, but the rest would have weighed the bag down."

"Wait. You said *bag*. Just one?"

"Yes..."

"*Ese maldito cabrón!*" the man swore, kicking the seat back before muttering, "*Se llevó la mitad.*"

Boone waited for more, but the man had returned to sullen silence. Sid was coming back across the road, several water bottles in his hands. Boone intercepted him. "I picked up a little Spanish in Curaçao. That bag of money and weaponry we found on the boat? Pretty sure there was a second bag in that compartment. Someone took it before we boarded."

"Did he tell you that?"

"Not in so many words. Your dad thinks there was another smuggler? I think he's right."

been rewarded. Sure enough, the couple went to the head of the stairs that led to the old customs house. The man checked the equipment in his pockets as he made a quick assessment: the girl had been a bit taller than he liked, but within the range of acceptable. The boy—*no…the young man*—had been in good shape. It would not be a sure thing. His instrument would be required.

Reverently, the Servant grasped the taped handle of the machete and headed for the gap in the wall.

———————— ◆ ·◆—————————

"I see the customs house," Emily called back to Lucky.

"OK, good." He grabbed a boat hook and joined her at the wheel, pointing to a spot ahead. "The buoy's right there. You get us moored and then suit up and enjoy the dive. I'll stay up top."

"Aye aye, Skipper." Emily took the pole and headed for the bow as Anika finished up the dive briefing.

"Remember, don't shine your lights directly on the fish—predators have learned to use that to target prey. If you see something you want to share, circle your beam of light *around* it. You'll find all sorts of things you won't see during the day. Moray eels come out to hunt, so you may spot some free-swimming through the coral. If you're lucky, you may see an octopus or two. And don't forget to look up from the coral from time to time—sometimes we get a school of Caribbean reef squid and they may give you a little light show. They flash patterns of color along their bodies to communicate. Any questions?" When no one replied, she clapped her hands together. "Good! Everybody take a moment to check your dive light again. I will have a spare … and I'll be the one with the little strobe hooked on my BC. If your light goes out, come find me. Gear up and we'll get started before the sun goes down."

Boone stepped to the dive platform to lower the ladder and check the current. The sea was still quite placid and as the boat came to rest on the mooring line, he could make out the bottom.

"Boone, you have a backup too, right?" Anika asked, joining him at the stern.

"Yeah. Actually, I've been using my backup as my primary. My main light is almost too bright for a tropical night dive."

"Don't you *dare* turn that thing on," Emily said, gearing up nearby. "His dive torch is ridiculous. That *cannon* will burn our retinas out and drive all the little squiddies away for miles around."

"In Bonaire, I tried it out and scared off a school of squid," Boone admitted to Anika.

"He *did*, the wanker. They were floating all around me. We were having a nice little chat!"

"Emily loves squid," Boone explained.

"I do!" Emily declared, breaking into song: "I love squid and squid love me and we'll have tea in the deep blue sea!"

The Wisconsin divers nearest the stern laughed at this spontaneous performance.

"You are certifiable," Boone said, shaking his head with a grin plastered on his face.

"Then I demand my certificate!"

"All right everyone, conditions look good," Anika announced. "Everybody in the pool."

"Lucky, you'll hold down the fort, yeah?" Emily called out.

"I'll be here," he said.

One by one, the divers turned on their lights and entered the water. As the sun kissed the horizon, they sank beneath the waves.

Well, they wasted no time, the Servant thought as grunts and moans rose from the small, white building. The customs house was little more than a tiny concrete shack topped with a red metal roof, doorless doorways on two sides and glassless windows on the other two. The sun had set several minutes before, and the shadows softened into a twilight gloom. Ten yards away, the Servant crouched in a stand of dense vegetation. The couple was clearly enjoying themselves, and as the sounds of rutting continued the Servant felt … *resentment*. He shook off the feeling, shifting his posture, keeping his muscles loose and warm. As the night grew closer, his eyes drifted to the light on the water far below. He had noticed the dive boat as he came down the path of stone stairs, trailing his quarry. A night dive, no doubt. He had done a fair amount of scuba diving himself in his time in the islands and knew it would be a shallow dive—likely over in an hour at most. He wasn't sure how far sound would carry, so he would have to wait.

The darkness grew. The sounds of passion crescendoed … then dissolved into merry laughter. Flashlights flicked on in the tiny building and the clink of beer bottles chimed in the night air. After a time, soft patches of glowing light played in the dark water near the distant dive boat as divers began to ascend.

Boone was the last to reach the surface, keeping up the rear and making sure all four Wisconsinites were accounted for. Emily and

Anika were already aboard, assisting the divers with their gear. Overhead, the night sky teemed with stars, the phosphorescent glow of the Milky Way arcing across a portion of it. This moment at the end of a night dive was one of Boone's favorite experiences in life, and here on the western side of Saba there were very few lights to spoil the view. Floating in the darkness, Boone glanced up at the dark cliffs of the island … and saw light. He squinted. The moon was just coming up in the south and would be full in a few days so he could just make out the customs house on the slope above. The light was coming from there, spilling out of a window on the wall facing the ocean. Every so often, a portion of the light would move. *Flashlights.* Boone watched a moment longer but found that his gaze had drifted to the side of the little building. To the shadows. A dark copse of foliage, no different than any other blob of shapes up on that slope. He shivered.

"Boone? You planning on joining us, or should we just leave you for my squid army to devour?"

"Wouldn't it be a squid navy?" Boone said, still looking up into the gloom, but swimming backward toward the *Shoal'Nuff.*

"You make a salient point," Emily replied. "But quit fannying around, I'm chilly."

Boone turned away from the dark shape of the island and ascended the ladder.

"What were you looking at?"

Boone pointed. "Couple flashlights in the customs house, I think."

Lucky joined them, helping Boone shed his tank to speed things along. "Probably some kids looking to fool around," he said. "We had a make-out place like that when I was growing up in Corpus Christi. Local playground. There was this little fort…"

11

"Well, it's official," Lucky said. "Irma is a hurricane." The Scenery Scuba dive staff were clustered around his laptop, looking at the latest from the National Hurricane Center website. "Sustained winds at 92 mph, pressure 983 millibars."

"Just a Category 1," Chad commented, referring to the Saffir-Simpson scale of hurricane categorization.

"Nearly a two, though," Emily said.

Lucky got up from his desk chair and stretched. "Considering the winds were just over sixty when I went to bed, that's pretty rapid intensification, 'specially for the overnight hours. But the track is still up in the air. Could miss us entirely. I'll talk to Lynn up at Sea Saba, see what they think. They have the most experience with this sort of thing. They dealt with Hurricane Lenny back in '99."

While Emily plopped into the empty chair and started looking through the latest advisory, Boone checked the chalkboard behind the desk. The afternoon was blank, but every slot for the morning was filled. "Looks like a full boat," he said.

"Yeah," Lucky said. "I'm thinking only one of you can go out with Anika and Chad today."

"Rock, paper, scissors!" Emily announced, popping up out of the chair. "One ... two ... *rock!*"

Boone had gone along with it and now held his flattened hand out, already grinning and shaking his head. He knew what came next.

"Bam, bam, bam!" Emily playfully battered Boone's "paper" hand. "Rock beats everything, Boone! You should know that by now."

Boone looked at the quizzical faces surrounding them. "It's, uh ... it's kind of a thing. Best to just roll with it."

"As always, you lose annnnnnd ... I'll stay," Emily said, flopping back into the chair and clicking on a satellite image of Irma. "I'm feeling a bit meteorological today."

Boone looked back at the chalkboard. At the end of the list of divers, he found two familiar names: Sid Every and Sophie Levenstone. "Sid and Sophie are diving today," he said. He turned to look at Emily and saw her suppressing a smile.

"I know. Anika already told me. We're besties now, haven't you heard?" She looked up from the computer. "Anika, I'm counting on you to keep my Boone safe from sharks, barracuda ... or any other kind of predator he might be swimming with."

Anika smiled and headed for the exit. "I'll make sure he's on his best behavior. We're back on the main pier, Boone. Help Chad bring the tanks."

"I've got a couple more to fill," Lucky said, and followed Chad to the fill room out back.

Boone lingered, stepping behind the desk. Emily studiously ignored him, clicking through screens on the laptop and smiling impishly. He knelt and spun her in the chair to face him, stopping her rotation with his hands on her thighs.

"Listen, Em … if you'd prefer—"

Emily grabbed his wrists and leaned forward abruptly, stopping his words with a sudden kiss. After a moment, she slowly withdrew. "Sorry. For a second there I thought you were going to make some tediously gallant offer to stay behind." She gave his cheek a playful slap. "You're a big boy, Boone. We had this talk, yeah? I'm just winding you up." She spun back to the laptop. "Now go show Sid and Sophie the wonders of the undersea world while I learn what a millibar is."

By nine o'clock the *Shoal 'Nuff* was motoring out of the enclosed bay, heading north to the leeward dive sites. As it turned out, the boat was not completely full after all.

"Sid was really looking forward to coming today. His ribs were feeling much better, so we both arranged to get the morning off for it. Even though he lives on an island, he hasn't dived very often." Sophie was sitting on a bench in a red bikini top, her wetsuit pulled up to her waist. She watched as Boone pulled on his own wetsuit.

"Police business, I'm guessing."

"Yes. Late last night, a family called saying their daughter hadn't come home. Then, early this morning, another call, another family. Their son wasn't in his bed when they woke up."

"The girl and boy … were they…?"

Sophie smiled. "Good instincts. Young and in love, is what Sid told me. He talked to several mutual friends of theirs and they all said they'd been dating for months. Maybe they eloped."

Boone nodded, mulling that over as he reached back and zipped up his suit.

Sophie stood, pulling up her own suit and threading her arms into the neoprene sleeves as she turned her back to Boone. "Can I get a zip?"

"Uh … sure."

"So … I'm going to need a dive buddy," Sophie said over her shoulder as Boone stepped behind her.

"Gotcha covered," Boone said, zipping her up. "Chad! Can you buddy up with Sophie?"

"It'd be my pleasure," Chad replied. "Don't you worry Sophie, you'll be in good hands."

Boone mouthed *sorry*, as Sophie gave him a look that promised future retribution. He left her to join Anika at the wheel. "Where to this morning?" he asked over the thrum of the engines.

"Diamond Rock," she said. "Up near the northwest coast. Still pretty calm, so it's a good day for it."

Ahead, a shape appeared in the distance. As they drew nearer, Boone could see it was an upthrust rock, tapering to a point, like a jagged tooth rising from the water. Adding to the toothy appearance was a predominately white coloration. Then, Boone noted the sea birds clustered at its apex. He stepped out from the cockpit to get a better look. Chad joined him.

"The white color … is that what I think it is?"

"If what you think it is is bird shit, then yes." Chad said. "This is a great dive, man, one of my faves. Pinnacle goes down to a sandy bottom at eighty feet so you can swim all around it. There're some great little canyons. A ton of spiny lobsters. I know where a little chain moray hangs out. If I spot it I'll try to catch your eye."

"I haven't seen many chains. Thanks."

"And thank *you* for my dive buddy." Chad winked and elbowed Boone, but then leaned in. "I'm just kidding, man. She's hot, but she's with Sid and he's a great guy. Besides, if I made a pass at her, she'd probably snap me in half."

"She might," Boone agreed, before grabbing the boat hook and mounting the bow, ready to snag the mooring line.

◆ ◆ ◆

After Diamond Rock, the dive boat had motored next door to Man O' War Shoals. Both dives had been spectacular, with far more life than on the previous days' dives. Boone had counted no less than eight juvenile drums on the last dive and made a mental note to insist Emily return here with her camera. The tiny black-and-white fish with its enormous trailing dorsal fin was one of her favorite underwater photography subjects.

"Hey, Boone..." Anika called, motioning him over to the wheel as they headed away from the mooring.

"What's up, 'Nika?" he asked.

"Emily for you," she said, handing her cell phone to him.

Boone pressed the phone to his ear, plugging the other with a finger. "Hello?"

"Boone, hey! I tried your cell first, but I'm guessing it's crammed into your dry bag. You survive the dives without me?"

"Barely. How about you? You learn everything you need to know to be a weather girl?"

"That's why I'm calling you. Hurricane Irma went through this bonkers intensification. She's up to 110 miles per hour. That's almost a Category 3."

"Just from this morning?"

"Yeah, totally off the trolley. The weather blokes are saying it's rare to ratchet up that fast."

"Is it coming here?"

"Still up in the air," Emily said. "So … how was diving with Sophie?"

"I buddied her up with Chad."

"Well I'll be jiggered, there's hope for you yet. Put Anika back on—Lucky wants to talk to her."

As the boat traveled south along the coast, Boone looked up and spotted the customs house in the distance. He thought back to last night: the flashlights. Maybe the missing boy and girl had been the ones with those lights. If so, perhaps they'd simply had a wild night and had turned up by now. *But you felt something else, didn't you?* His eyes locked onto the little building's white walls and red roof, tracking it as the boat swept past, heading back toward Fort Bay.

✦ • ✦

"Where is it?" the Servant snarled. He dug through his belongings for the third time. After a moment, he stopped and took several long, slow breaths. *You probably lost it last night. Where? Think back.*

It had been a long night, and he was exhausted. The girl had regained consciousness as he was binding her with duct tape. She had given him a nasty set of scratches on his neck before he could subdue her, holding her still while he injected her with a dose of the sedative he had stolen from a medical school on a previous island. Then the long trek up the stone stairs to the cottage, the girl over his shoulder. He had stopped from time to time, listening intently, in the unlikely event someone else was out for a nighttime hike. After chaining her in the basement of the cottage, another trip back down to the customs house to dispose of the body. The sleeping bag made a convenient means of conveyance, and he had loaded the corpse into it alongside the flashlights, beer bottles, and the bloody rags and cleaning supplies he had used to wipe up the blood. Fortunately, most of it had been absorbed by the sleeping bag and the young man's T-shirt. It had taken nearly an hour for the Servant to bring the heavier load up to the top of the stairs.

Then had come the trickiest part. The Servant didn't want to risk carrying the body out in the open, but the road was the only safe way to get to the trail he had scouted yesterday morning. Leaving the sleeping bag near the base of the stairs, he went to the cottage and backed his SUV to the break in the wall, loading the sleeping bag onto a tarp in the back. Driving slowly with the lights off, he parked at the dead end. The nearby residence was completely dark and he quickly unloaded the sleeping bag, stuffing the tarp into it before starting carefully down Middle Island Trail. Even with his tremendous strength, carrying this kind of load down a steep, uneven trail in near darkness was a difficult task. He had taken his time and was grateful that the bright glow of the waxing moon had illuminated the way. It would be full in just six days. This was a fact he knew very well.

Reaching the abandoned cistern he'd found yesterday, the Servant loaded the now-bulging sleeping bag with a number of sizeable rocks. He stripped out of his coveralls and stuffed them in as well. Finally, zipping the bag shut, he pitched it into the brackish water where it immediately sank. The cool night air felt glorious on his sweat-soaked body as he climbed back up the trail, nude but for the hiking boots on his feet and several leather thongs around his neck. After insuring the coast was clear, he quickly ran to the truck, grabbing a pair of clean coveralls from the passenger seat. He had been wise to buy these in bulk during his time in Nevis.

It was nearly dawn by the time he returned to the cottage basement and collapsed onto a folding cot to sleep, the whimpers of his prisoner mingling with his soft snores. Upon waking, he had reached up to the thongs on his neck, his fingers finding the items threaded through the lengths of leather: a musket ball from Saint Kitts, a shark's tooth from Nevis, a chunk of pumice from Montserrat … but that was all. One was missing. The Servant had spent several minutes retracing his steps in his mind.

Now, breathing slowly, his fingers rose again to the thongs around his neck. This time they paused as they found the spot where his prisoner had scratched him. He opened his eyes and slowly turned to the girl in the corner of the basement, her wrists handcuffed behind her back, the cuffs themselves secured to a sturdy pipe. "You…" he growled. The girl saw the look in his eyes and shrank from him, scooting back along the earthen floor. The pipe only allowed a few inches of retreat and she whimpered into the duct tape layered across her mouth. The brief struggle just outside the customs house when she revived from the choke hold—she must have snagged the missing thong when she clawed at his face. Rage building, the man took two steps toward her.

And stopped in his tracks. The Voice came to him. A tiny part of his rational mind knew it was only his own thoughts, but the greater part of him believed that voice was so much more, springing from ancient places. *No. You may not harm her further. She no longer belongs to you. You will keep her safe, to fulfill her greater purpose.*

The man relaxed, his face awash with a sudden calm. "Of course. So it shall be," he said aloud into the musty air of the basement. He would wait for dark and return to the customs house. He would find his missing talisman. Right now, he needed to prepare for a trip to town to meet with the forger. He smiled at the terrified girl. "I imagine you're thirsty. Hungry too. I'll fetch you something. You'll need to keep your strength up."

———————◆•◆———————

"Sid!" Boone called out. He had asked Sophie to drop him and Emily at the police station in The Bottom before she headed to the airport for her afternoon shift.

Sid turned from the police vehicle he was exiting. "Hey, Boone! How was the diving? Sorry I couldn't make it."

"Next time," Boone said. "Sid, the missing couple ... did they show up?"

"Not yet," Sid said. "I just got back from Immigration at Fort Bay. Checked the passenger manifest for the morning ferry. I thought that maybe they'd snuck off to Saint Martin, but no luck there. Dad's doing the same down at the airport."

"Sid ... can you take me to the customs house?"

"What? Why?"

Boone explained what he had seen the night before, giving the approximate time and the fact that there were two flashlights.

"The customs house ... why didn't I think of that?" Sid said. "Yeah, I heard that used to be the place to go catawowing about." He held up a hand. "Sorry. Saban expression. Means fooling around."

Boone started to say more, but stopped.

"Go on, Boone," Emily prompted. On the drive up, he had told her of the odd sense of foreboding he had felt.

"Sid ... I just have this feeling that there's something more to it than a couple kids fooling around."

"What do you mean?" Sid asked.

Boone looked uncomfortable but Emily stepped in. "Boone has these ... *feelings* sometimes. I've learned to roll with it. He's usually right."

Sid didn't hesitate. "Hop in," he said, opening the doors to the police car.

12

The man known locally as "Wink" stared intently at the passport, peering through an oversized magnifying glass. The Servant stood patiently to the side, glancing around the tiny room hidden in the back of the cottage. Wink looked up. "Gunter Schleich," he said. "Do he want da same name, or another one?"

"New name, new address," the Servant said, retrieving a folded paper from a pocket of his crisp new coveralls and handing it to Wink.

Wink took it and read through the paper's contents, his right eye occasionally twitching. He'd had the nervous tic since childhood, hence his nickname. "Yours won't be difficult—I have what I need to make de adjustments to an American passport. But if your friend wants a new EU passport, dere is a different method to da holographic security strip and I'll need to involve my partner in Saint Martin. And it will cost double."

The Servant nodded. He wouldn't be paying for it. He'd pick up the additional funds tomorrow when he delivered the water Gunter had requested. "How long before I can get it?" he asked.

The man "chupsed", sucking his teeth as he thought for a moment. The Servant had heard chupsing often, an odd but common cultural habit among many islanders, meant to express a variety of emotions. Finally, Wink spoke. "Dere's a ferry to Saint Martin tomorrow afternoon. I have a runner I can send. And I'm expecting a friend wit' a boat to make a delivery to Saint Martin later in da weekend. He can bring da papers back and I can finish up by..." The eye twitched in a flurry. "Sunday night. Best I can do."

"All right."

"Anyt'ing else?"

The man removed a small vial from a pocket. "I need more of this. I imagine the Medical School has some?"

Wink peered at the label. "Not possible. Dat sort of thing would be under lock and key and I don't have no one on de inside. Sorry."

The Servant thought about asking if some could be procured from Saint Martin, but after running some numbers in his head he decided against it. It would be unnecessarily costly, and he had enough to last until the night it would no longer be needed. As long as he had sufficient doses to keep his prisoner quiet when he left the house, he could make do.

Wink made a shooing motion. "Come back Sunday mornin'. I need to make some calls right now to make sure we can get it by den. I hear tell dere may be a hurricane coming, and my runner will want to have his boat safely berthed in case we get a blow."

The Servant frowned. "What hurricane?"

"Dey calling her Irma."

A flash of red roof through the low trees and the customs house came into view below. It was much smaller than Boone had expected. "Not exactly a stately government building," he observed.

"Didn't have to be," Sid responded. "Just a bit of shelter for a customs officer to be stationed. Hasn't seen any use since the main pier went in at Fort Bay."

"You ever bring a girl here, Sid?"

"No. I was actually in the States for my education after middle school, but I've heard teens and college students sometimes come up here. My dad said he did when he was young. I don't think it happens all that often, though. Can't really leave your car along Ladder Hill Road, and it's a long hike to get here."

As they reached the building, Boone began to look around. It was after four and the sun was still bright on this western slope. The rough stone steps angled around to the right of the customs house, and off to the left were a couple concrete blocks. One was upright, hollow and shaped like an outhouse, while the other might have been a cistern. Short of the main building, Boone stopped, staring at a thick clump of brush. Emily came up beside him.

"Something there?" she asked softly.

Boone shook his head. "No. Not now, at least. I don't know…" He approached the little concrete landing at the nearest opening into the customs house and looked inside. Just an empty rectangular room with another doorway across and an empty window on either side. A single cabinet, its light blue paint peeling, sat against the wall on the upslope side. Boone looked to his right at the sparkling sea. *That's where we were night diving.* He walked around the building, noting a little plaque that spoke about the history of The Ladder.

"You said you saw one light leave the building?" Sid's voice came from inside.

"Yes," Boone said, continuing around and up a little rise into some bushes. "Over here, I think." He looked around, but nothing caught his eye.

"Couple bottlecaps here," Emily called out from inside the customs house. "Carib."

"Popular beer on Saba, a close second to Heineken," Sid remarked. "Those could be from any time."

"Could ... but they look pretty shiny to me," Emily observed. "And you know how fast things rust near the sea."

Sid took one of the yellow discs. "You're right," he said, then gave it a sniff. "And I wouldn't swear to it, but..."

Emily sniffed the other. "Smells beery to me. Boone, you want to join the party and get a whiff?"

He didn't hear her. He had approached the other doorway and his eyes were drawn to the floor just inside. Sid started to speak, but Emily squeezed his arm and put a finger to her lips. After a moment, Boone blinked and looked at them. "Does that patch of floor look clean to you?"

Sid looked down. "It's all pretty dirty in here, if you ask me."

"No ... I mean clean*er*. Step back and look at the whole floor."

They did so and Emily nodded. "Yeah ... I mean ... *maybe?*"

"You know what I think?" Sid asked, as he took a Ziploc from a pocket and dropped the bottle caps into it. "Our missing couple may have been here last night but they're not here now. I think I should canvass the cottages up on Ladder Hill Road, see if anyone saw anything unusual."

They headed out the doorway to the steps. Sid and Emily began to climb, but Boone lingered, letting his eyes go unfocused as he took in the whole scene: the customs house, the steps, the sea. He turned and headed after his friends before stopping dead in his tracks. *Something out of place. Something blue.* He went back and walked right up to a patch of rich soil and tropical roots just to the side of the steps, not three feet from the entrance to the customs house. *There.* Under the roots, looking like a thin root itself, was a length of leather threaded through a small object. Gingerly, he picked it up. A leather cord necklace. One end was curled, the knot having pulled open. Threaded through the cord was a small object. Cobalt blue, it appeared to be made of hard pottery. *No … it's glass.* It was five-sided, its edges worn smooth.

"What did you find?" Emily asked, having followed him back down.

"A necklace of some kind." He showed them where he'd found it.

"I think that's a slave bead," Sid said. "Can I see it?" Sid slid the bead off of the cord and examined it. "Yes, it is. Well, they call them 'blue beads' now. They come from Sint Eustatius, the island next door. The Dutch used to give them to the slaves as a form of currency. Someone is going to be furious," he said, threading it back on the cord. "These are becoming quite rare."

"You could ask the parents of the missing boy and girl, see if it belongs to either of them," Emily suggested.

"Good idea," Sid said.

"Actually…" Boone began. "Um … this is going to sound silly, but … do you mind if I hang onto that for a bit?"

Sid frowned. "Why?"

Boone shook his head, looking sheepish. "Honest answer? I have no idea." When Sid hesitated, Boone continued. "Look, I'm not gonna do a seance with it or anything. I just think it might spark an idea. Or not." He sighed. "Never mind. It's pretty silly."

"Oh, what the hell," Sid said, digging his phone out. "Here, hold the bead up," he said, handing the necklace to Boone and snapping a picture on his smart phone. "All right, here's the deal. Ninety percent chance a tourist probably dropped that, so go

13

"All right, gather 'round," Lucky said. He and Emily were peering at the latest weather report and Anika, Chad, and Boone joined them at the desk.

"How does it look?" Anika asked.

"Still a Cat 3," Emily said. "Winds ticked up a notch to 115 mph."

"The problem is, the track is tightening a bit," Lucky said. "I talked to Sea Saba and they've decided to take their boats across to Saint Martin for safe keeping on Sunday. If we get hit, anything in Fort Bay is likely to get wrecked."

"So, you planning to take the *Shoal 'Nuff* to Saint Martin, too?" Boone asked. "With her engine just fixed, I don't know…"

"I had the same thought. But one of the advantages of her being small, I can hook her up on a trailer and bring her up to The Bottom. Got a buddy with an empty lot who will let me store her there. So, plan is … last dives are today and tomorrow. Then we'll secure the boat and the store. Although, hopefully Miss Irma will decide to take a tour of the Atlantic instead."

The first morning dive at Shark Shoals had gone well and they were coming to the end of their second morning dive at Rays n' Anchors, closer to Fort Bay. Boone was nearing his safety stop below the surface, a watchful eye on the divers in his charge. Chad was manning the boat and Anika was already aboard. The sound of a boat engine, moving at speed, caught his ear. Above, the *Shoal 'Nuff* was still on the mooring line so Boone began to look around. Emily was further off to the side and she caught his eye, pointing two fingers at her mask, then pointing to the south. *Look there.* Sure enough, the underside of a boat came into view, the engines throttling down to an idle as it coasted toward the dive boat. Boone was relieved it was staying well clear of the stern, where the divers were ascending. The Diver Down flag would be displayed, so the newcomer should know to keep their distance.

Boone kicked toward Emily, leveling off at fifteen feet. Checking his computer, he began the three-minute safety stop to allow some of the accumulated nitrogen in his body to dissipate. Emily checked her computer as well, floating effortlessly at the precise depth. Looking over to Boone, she mimed a Rockettes dance kick, pumping her fists and kicking a fin to alternating sides, ending with a bow. Boone clapped as Emily mimed kisses to the audience before a shrill *bee-dee-deep* from her computer informed her the three minutes were up. Waving goodbye, she headed for the surface. Boone followed.

Once on deck, Boone could see the other vessel was a small fishing boat with a sizeable pair of outboards. Its captain was a dark-skinned islander, his hair speckled with white, and his thin frame wiry and weathered. It was hard to tell how old he was, but he clearly had some mileage on him. He was calling across to Chad in an island sing-song.

"No, no, I gots to get back to Statia before dat bitch Irma pays us a visit. Soon as I do my bidness in Saint Martin, I head straight back. You lucky I run into you. Good to see you, Chad! Pleasure, as always."

"You too, Reynaldo!" Chad replied, waving.

"Wait!" Boone had a flash of memory and went to the gunwale. A smuggler in Bonaire whom Boone had been friendly with had given him the name of a Statian he should look up. "Reynaldo!" The man was about to throttle up but paused, turning back to the *Shoal 'Nuff.* Boone held a hand up in greeting. "Do you know a Darcy DaSilva?"

Reynaldo looked surprised, though that look slipped into one of wariness. "Who you?" he called.

"Boone Fischer. Friend of Darcy's. I knew him in Bonaire. He gave me your name when he heard I was coming here."

Reynaldo nodded, thinking for a moment before calling out again. "Come over for a visit. I run you back to Fort Bay."

"Anika, do you mind?"

"No, we're done for today. Just leave your gear and pick it up when you get back."

"Thanks. Em, care to—"

"See you over there!" Emily had already stripped off her gear and dived into the water, sunglasses firmly in hand, her lime green shorty vanishing beneath the waves before she knifed back to the surface and slid her ever-present shades onto her face. Boone dived in after her and they reached Reynaldo's boat just as he hooked a simple wooden ladder onto the transom.

"Welcome aboard *Da Breez,*" he said as they climbed up. He laughed when they stood side by side on the deck. He turned his hands palms-down and held them out flat, one high, one low, indicating their widely differing heights. "Hoo! Gyul, he like two of you."

"Yeah, but *here*, I'm like two of him," Emily said without skipping a beat, pointing a finger at her head.

Reynaldo nodded appreciatively. "Bet you are, bet you are. And what is your name, beautiful lady?"

"Emily Durand," she replied, offering her hand. Reynaldo took it and shook it.

"*Very* pleased to meet you. And you too, Boone. I'm Reynaldo, but ever'one call me Rey. So, you know Darcy, uh? He still have dat silly boat? What he call it?"

"The *Yachty McYachtface*," Emily said, mirth coloring her voice.

"Yeah, dat's it! Ha! Yeah, me and him do a little business in Dominica from time to time. So … you need somet'ing?"

"Like what?" Boone asked, unzipping his wetsuit and stripping the top part off his arms and chest, leaving it to dangle from his waist.

"Like … well, you tell me." Reynaldo trailed off and looked at Boone. "You know what Darcy do for a living?"

"Yes … he's an independent maritime contractor," Boone said, remembering Darcy's own euphemism for his smuggling activities.

"Oh, dat's good, I'll have to remember dat one," Reynaldo said, smiling for a moment before looking cagey again. "You meant smuggler, right?"

Boone laughed. "Yes, I did. But no, we don't need anything. I just heard your name, heard you mention Statia, and remembered Darcy telling me about you."

"You been to Statia yo'self, I see." Reynaldo said.

"Well, we stopped at the airport over there on the way to Saba," Boone said. "But that's it."

"Den where you get da blue bead?"

Boone's fingers found the smooth object at the hollow of his throat. He'd forgotten he'd had it on under the wetsuit. He explained how he'd come to possess it, searching for clues of the missing couple.

Reynaldo nodded sagely. "It's good da policeman let you keep it. Dey say you don't find da blue bead, da blue bead find you. Don't ever sell it. Bad luck." He raised a bony wrist and waggled a leather bracelet. On it were three Statian beads. "I could probably get a t'ousand dollars for dese, but I'd never sell."

"Oh, I'll probably have to give this one back ... I just wanted to wear it for a while."

"I'm suddenly feeling very bead bereft," Emily said.

"Come to Statia some time, maybe a bead will find you," Reynaldo said. "Dese missing young ones, I hope dey turn up. We had a girl go missing on Statia. No one knows what happened to her. I know one of her friends—she in a dark place."

"When was this?" Boone asked.

"Just last month," Reynaldo said. "Very pretty girl. Tiny, like you," he added, gesturing to Emily.

Back in Fort Bay, Boone and Emily headed for the *Shoal 'Nuff* to get their gear as Reynaldo motored off to the north, vanishing around the western cliffs. Anika and Chad had already left, but Lucky was still there, typing away at his laptop.

"Cancelling some upcoming dive packages. I ain't gonna lie, this is gonna hurt my wallet. Already let Anika and Chad go for the day."

"Anything we can do?" Boone asked. "No charge."

"Actually, can you take my car and grab some grub for me? My Texas teeth are craving a burger and Island Flavor has a great one. Get yourselves something too." He scrounged up two twenties and handed them over with his keys.

Up in The Bottom, they ordered a trio of burgers. While they cooked up, they headed around the corner to the police station to see if Sid was in. His father met them at the front desk.

"Sid's up at the annex in Windwardside. Can I pass something along?"

"Actually, sir ... just as well I tell *you*. Did Sid explain this?" Boone indicated the bead.

"Yes. A Statian Blue Bead. We ran the photo by the parents of the missing couple. It didn't belong to either of them. Sid was right—probably dropped by a tourist."

"Well, that might be but ... I just talked to a Statian. He said they had a girl go missing over there last month."

"Really? Huh. What was the Statian's name?"

"Didn't catch it," Boone said, not knowing the exact extent of Reynaldo's activities. "I think you should reach out to the Statian police. Compare notes."

"Well ... we haven't had much luck, so I'll take any lead I can get. I'll give them a call. I know most of them over there."

"Sid was going to canvass the neighbors up by The Ladder," Emily said. "Any luck?"

"No. Only two of the cottages are occupied at the moment and they didn't see anything out of the ordinary. A grocery store in The Bottom remembered them buying Carib beer that evening."

"I think they were at the customs house," Boone said.

"So do I," Captain Every replied.

14

"What's the latest on the weather, Anika?" Boone asked as he set his gear into a niche and stood dripping beside the stern ladder to await the divers below. The Wisconsinites had flown home and Scenery Scuba had a new group of three divers from New York this morning. Emily and Chad were still down there with them and Boone watched their bubbles as Anika joined him.

"Same as this morning. Irma is weaker, down to a two, and the track looks about fifty-fifty for us. If it hooks north of Barbuda, we'll be fine. So far, no watches or warnings."

"But I'm guessing we'll be bringing the boat out of the water as planned."

"Oh, absolutely. Besides, at this point, Lucky has already processed cancellations, and tourists will be cramming into the ferries and onto the last WinAir flights. Even if it misses us, there won't be anyone here to go diving with!"

An outstretched hand breached the waves as the first diver surfaced, tapping her head to indicate everything was okay, then kicked to the ladder where Boone waited to accept her fins. In minutes, everyone was aboard, Chad bringing up the rear.

"Anika!" he called out. "Can we stay moored and take the surface interval here? There are some *monster* lionfish down there."

"How's your deco load?" Boone asked, referring to the residual nitrogen in Chad's blood.

Chad paused on the ladder and glanced at his integrated computer. "I'm just in the yellow. And plenty in the tank."

"I don't know..." Anika said.

He scrambled up the ladder and headed for his gear bag. "Oh, c'mon! Just down and back. With the storm coming in, the restaurants are going to run out of lionfish. They pay good money, and cash is going be a little tight this week. There are three under one overhang, only sixty feet down." He was already retrieving his cylindrical lionfish trap, clipping it to the side of his BC with a pair of carabiners, so that it rested against his hip. "Second dive, I'll stay on the boat." He grabbed two silver gloves from his gear bag and slid them on.

"Is that ... chain mail?" Melissa, one of the New Yorkers, asked.

"Kinda, yeah," Chad stepped over to the girl to show her. "Sometimes the reefies get a bit aggressive and go for the lionfish on your spear. Just a precaution." He hefted the pole spear, the head tipped with a cluster of three barbed points and the butt end sporting a simple loop of rubber tubing. "So, I take this spear and pull it back like this, see?" He demonstrated, looping the band on his hand and lightly gripping the spear. He stretched the elastic band taut, pointing the triple barbs over the gunwale. "Then you just ... let go." Chad released his grip and the spear shot forward through his curled fingers. "Then you stuff the lionfish in your trap." He held up the end of the white, plastic tube at his side and pushed the spear tips into it. "This end cap on the tube bends *in*, but it won't bend out. You stick it in, and then you … pull out." He grinned at Melissa and sat on the gunwale to don his fins.

"Well, I suppose—" Anika began, but Chad was already rolling backward into the water.

"Boone," Emily said, leaning in close to him. He bent down a bit so she could speak in his ear. "I counted five reef sharks down there."

Boone nodded, having already decided. He grabbed his mask and fins.

"I could go," Anika said, although she was dressed for the boat and Chad might be back before she got suited up.

"No, no, I'll go," Boone said.

"You want the spare tank?" Anika asked.

"I'll freedive it."

Anika just nodded, but the New Yorker nearest the stern looked incredulous. "What? No tank? He said it was sixty feet down!"

"Sixty is nothing for Boone," Emily said, a touch of pride in her voice.

"Well, it's not *nothing*," Boone said. "I don't know how long he'll be, so I might have to return for another breath."

"Won't you get the bends?" another diver asked.

"Normally, no—freediving doesn't put any nitrogen in your blood—but since I just dived, it could be an issue. I'll probably need to hang out at the safety stop. Actually … hey, Em, can you weight a tank and drop it down on a line? Like we had on the chain on our boat in Bonaire?"

"Brill idea," she said, grabbing her BC and tank. "I've still got a thousand in mine and the BC has integrated weights. Have it down in a jiff."

"Can I borrow your weight belt?" Boone asked Melissa. She handed it to him, and he quickly stripped off two of the weights, leaving a pair of two-pounders. Strapping it on his waist, he pulled on his fins and hopped into the water beside the ladder. Ducking his mask underwater, he looked down to see Chad approaching a ridge of coral. Raising his head and hooking an arm on the ladder, Boone relaxed his body and cleared his mind, taking slow, deep breaths through his mouth, making each exhalation four times as long as the inhalation to decrease his heart rate. After a minute, he took one final deep breath, feeling his ribs expand as he filled his lungs to capacity. Releasing the ladder, he slipped beneath the waves. A splash nearby signaled the arrival of Emily's impromptu safety-stop air.

Back in Bonaire, the Rock Beauty Divers boat had a weighted chain that could be lowered over the side with a regulator on a long hose rigged to a spare tank above. In practice, they only deployed it for deep sites and few divers ever used it. As Boone let himself drift a bit deeper, he saw a pair of reef sharks off to the left, probably at about seventy feet. Chad was inverted, looking under a shelf, no doubt trying to locate his lionfish honey hole. Suddenly, he kicked away from the shelf and oriented himself upright, drawing the spear back, the elastic band pulling taut. The tip darted under the shelf and when Chad withdrew it a sizeable lionfish was impaled on its barbed points, its long pectoral fins and poisonous spines extended to either side. With practiced ease, Chad popped the fish into the tube and lined his spear up for another strike.

Boone's eye was drawn to movement. A reef shark banked sharply, heading toward Chad. Kicking his fins, Boone headed down to fifty feet. Chad's spear struck again, and the reef shark dipped its pectoral fins and snapped its tail, increasing its speed to a sprint. Boone picked up speed as well. In the peripheral vision to his right, two more reef sharks shed their slow, graceful movements for more abrupt shifts in direction, agitated by the death throes of the fish on the spear points.

Chad pushed the second lionfish into his tube and quickly speared the third, rising from the ledge to head back to the boat. Seeing Boone, he raised the impaled lionfish, showing off his kill. That was when the first reefy struck. With a final burst of speed, it snapped the lionfish right off of the spear, dashing for the blue. One of the other reef sharks peeled off after it, the other continuing to approach Chad. Now, from the left, another reef shark appeared, swimming in erratic half-circles. Boone estimated it to be nearly seven feet long. Realizing that Chad's tube still held two bleeding lionfish, he jerked a thumbs-up symbol at Chad, pumping it three times. *Ascend now!* The Californian signaled *OK* and began to rise.

Boone knew he probably had only a minute, maybe a minute and a half, before he'd run out of oxygen and begin to gray out. He also knew that a "shallow water blackout" could strike quite suddenly. Kicking hard, he headed to the dangling tank. Looking back, he saw a smaller reefy abruptly turn away as Chad poked his spear at it. Boone reached the air supply and took the regulator in his mouth, breathing in and out several times, doing his best to remain calm even in the current situation. His eyes locked onto the larger reef shark. It wove back and forth, then cut sharply away from Chad. Boone breathed easier and Chad saw the change in direction too, flashing another OK sign as he rose to thirty feet in depth, taking his time now. Ascending too rapidly was a good way to get decompression sickness and win a no-expenses-paid trip to the hyperbaric chamber.

Then the shark turned back. Boone sucked in a rib-straining lungful of air, pointing at the shark with several jabs of his finger. Chad turned, bringing his spear up in time to arrest its approach. It swung to its left, moving away … then suddenly whipped its head to the right, coming in on Chad's flank, mouth opening and upper teeth protruding as it snapped its jaws at the lionfish tube dangling against the Californian's hip. It missed the tube … but found a leg instead.

Boone inverted and shot toward Chad, his mind already working on a course of action. Contrary to Hollywood creature features, sharks were not mindless eating machines, and the reefy clearly wasn't expecting the mouthful it had gotten. It broke off from Chad, circling, jaws working as it debated what it had tasted. From the tendril of blood streaming back from the corner of its mouth and the spreading cloud at the Californian's side, it was clear it had tasted Chad. Reaching the stricken diver in seconds, Boone grabbed the tube with the two speared lionfish inside. In the distance, the seven-foot reef shark turned. Chad had rigged a couple straps to the tube and Boone released the nearest carabiner, his fingers scrambling for the second one as the blunt nose of the reefy rocketed in. Unclipping the second carabiner, he held the tube at arm's length and swept it to the side, releasing it just as the reef shark clamped the cylinder in its jaws.

Boone gripped Chad and kicked for the surface, putting his mask to Chad's own. He was relieved to see there was no panic in his eyes—although that could be the onset of shock. Boone saw the lionfish spear slip from Chad's fingers and he instinctively shot his hand out, grabbing it before it could sink to the bottom, his thoughts rushing by in a flurry. *Grab it! Might need it … aannnnnnd yep, gonna need it. Two smaller sharks coming in. Okay, one's turning away. Oh, you're not? Here's a poke in the nose for you then, Mr. Shark. Good, that worked. How deep are we? Less than twenty, I think. Man, that's a lot of blood. There's the boat, fifteen feet, kick for the ladder, oh good, there's Emily. Plenty of air, don't black out, don't black out, don't—*

◆ ◆ ◆

When Boone came to, the first thing he saw was … *himself.* Two of himself.

"Boone, wake up! Boone!" Emily's voice came from the dual images of his face and he realized he was looking into her sunglasses. He felt a gentle rocking sensation, and waves lapped at his ears. Suddenly, he sucked in a gulp of air as his body decided he was no longer underwater and it was safe to breathe again.

"Oh thank God!" Emily was cradling his head above the water with a grip in his hair, one of her legs wrapped around his body, the other leg and arm holding them both against the ladder.

"Chad?"

"He's in the boat. They're stopping the bleeding."

"How long was I…?"

"About five seconds. You passed out just as you got to the surface. Can you get up the ladder? We've got to go now!"

"Yeah…" His fuzzy thoughts were quickly sharpening, the effects of the shallow water blackout dissipating quickly. Not wanting to bother with his fins, he reached up and grabbed hold of the top rungs, his wiry muscles pulling him up and out of the water. He swung onto the swim platform, stripping off the fins as Emily climbed up the ladder after him. On the deck, two of the New Yorkers were pressing a rapidly reddening towel to the side of Chad's thigh. The injured diver's face was very pale.

Anika jumped down into the cockpit, tossing the pole hook aside as she turned the key, bringing the engines to life. "Emily! Grab my phone on the dash. Dial 911. Faster than the radio to get the paramedics down to the bay. Boone! Ladder!"

Boone quickly swung up the bottom half of the ladder on its hinge and fastened it in place.

"Everybody, hang on to something!" Anika yelled.

15

The Servant paused to look down at the sea below. A single
rock jutted out of the waves, a small amount of greenery on
its flattened top. He remembered the map had called it Green
Island. Shifting the heavy backpack on his shoulders, he started
down the steep slope. Though on an incline, this part was surprisingly flat, the ground covered in short, brownish grass. It almost
looked like a Midwestern prairie—if that prairie sat at a forty-five
degree angle. Nearing the edge of the cliff, he looked to his right
and could make out the tiny landing strip of the Saba airport,
perched on a tiny plateau. He had not arrived on this island by
air, but he had heard that the take-offs and landings were legendary. Beside him was a wooden sign, painted in faded white-
and-green, one arrowed edge pointing the way to what the green
lettering spelled out in all caps: SULPHUR MINE. Stepping off
the low grass, he followed a gravel-strewn trail along the edge
of the cliffs overhead until the entrance to the mine came into
view. It was a small cave opening, the mouth of a tunnel, but *hole*

was the word that came to mind when he looked at it. An oval of black in a canvas of dusty gray.

He approached the mouth of the mine and shrugged off the backpack. He remembered how low the ceiling was at the opening; the backpack would likely scrape the rocks overhead. Walking in a crouch, the Servant entered the mine. The sunlight from outside didn't reach far and soon he had to stop, setting down the backpack to dig the headlamp out of a pocket. Those he served had blessed him with excellent night vision but in another twenty feet it would be pitch black. Securing the lamp's band to his head, the Servant noted his hair was already drenched in sweat. The air in here was stifling! Switching on the headlamp, he bent to retrieve the backpack, scraping against the side wall as he did so. The walls were close, such that two men would not be able to walk abreast. At least the ceiling was a little higher here, though he still had to bend slightly, given his height. The headlamp's beam caught sparkles on the walls and he leaned in, peering at the substance. Grazing two fingertips against the mustard-yellow material, he played his fingers in the light. *Sulphur.* One of the holy substances those he served brought up from the Great Below. Wiping his hand on his coveralls, he continued deeper into the mine.

He reached an intersection, the right tunnel plunging down an incline, the left remaining relatively level. Taking the left, he soon came to an iron grating, painted yellow, set into the mouth of a side tunnel. A padlock joined two of the thin bars, sealing shut what passed for a gate. This had been where the Servant had met the smuggler before. Beyond the barrier was a room, several dust-encrusted tools and buckets lying in the corners like historical artifacts. At the back of the room, another tunnel extended as far as the headlamp's beam could reach.

"Gunter?" The Servant's voice echoed off the walls. Nothing. "Gunter, I have your water. And news." Still nothing. The smuggler had told him that if he didn't want to be found, the Servant would never find him. *Perhaps he's playing a game with me. Or perhaps, he's simply somewhere else.* Turning away from the gate, he headed deeper into the mine. It was at this point that the heat began to build, seeming to jump thirty degrees in as many feet. The rotten egg smell that had been barely evident before was stronger here. The Servant smiled. *And some say this one is extinct.* This place … it was *ripe*, just waiting for his arrival. Clicking off his headlamp, he set down the backpack, carefully straightening until his hair brushed the low ceiling. Reaching out to either side, he pressed the palms of his powerful hands against the walls of the tunnel, feeling the mineral deposits compress under his skin. Standing in the pitch black, breathing slowly in the sweltering reek, the Servant pictured the tunnel ahead burrowing down, down, down into the mountain. His mind sank deeper still. He pictured the magma flowing below, like the blood in the veins of the earth itself, connecting this place of power with many others nearby. Unbidden, he felt a spark of arousal stir within him. Perhaps *this* time. Perhaps this sacrifice would finally serve to awaken them. *But, if not this time … then another … there would always be another cycle.*

"Hey! Come back to the gate!" a heavily accented voice echoed in the darkness. "I vanted to be sure you veren't followed."

Switching on the headlamp, the Servant lifted the backpack and returned the way he had come. When the gate came into view, he slowed his advance. He knew Gunter didn't trust him. That was only reasonable—he didn't trust the smuggler, either. Nonetheless, they each had their usefulness to the other. Taking one step at a time, the Servant approached the gate, his headlamp gradually illuminating the space beyond. The tunnel at the back of the little room was just at the limits of the headlamp, but as he took one more step, he could make out a dark shape crouched in the gloom of that tunnel. It was Gunter. And he was armed. It was difficult to tell, but it appeared to be an assault rifle of some kind.

"Halt! Far enough," the smuggler said. The Servant caught a glint at the level of the man's eyes and could just make out a set of night-vision goggles. "Rotate your headlamp to the back of your head. This vill give you enough light und I von't have to stare into *die verdammte* thing."

The Servant set the backpack down and did as the man asked. Enough light reflected off the walls that he could still make out the metal bars and see a short distance into the room beyond.

The smuggler coughed, the sound coming from the gloom. "The air. It stinks more some days than others."

"I have your water."

"Set it by the grating."

The Servant extracted the case of two dozen bottles of water, the plastic wrapping enclosing the pallet crackling as he dragged it out. He set it on the ground near the padlock. He tipped the backpack forward, holding it open so Gunter could see inside, then withdrew two plastic grocery bags full of fruit, bread, and a few canned items. "I brought you some additional food. You may be here longer than you thought."

"Vat? Vhy? Is there a problem vit the passport?"

"That's part of it. The forger needed to outsource to someone with experience in EU passports. He requires another two thousand for this added expense. It will be available tomorrow night at the earliest. I will deliver them the next day, when I am able. And I will expect the remaining $11,000 at that time."

"You vill have it. But if I vill have the papers two days from now, das is not so bad. Vhy did you say—"

"There is a hurricane on the way."

"*Scheisse*. Do they think it vill hit Saba?" He pronounced the island's name "SAH-buh," the way many Europeans did.

"It may. They are still not sure. But there is enough of a chance that the ferries and planes will be full, and the port will be cleared of boats. It may be some time before you can arrange to leave safely."

"Vat about you?" the smuggler asked.

The Servant smiled. "I'm right where I want to be."

"He should be fine," the Saban doctor said to the group in the waiting room of the A. M. Edwards Medical Center. Sighs of relief emanated from everyone assembled. "It was just a test bite. Unfortunately, from the look of it—and from what Boone described—it was a fairly large shark, so there was a lot of blood loss."

Lucky shook his head. "It's crazy! I looked it up." He held up his smartphone, turning the screen to face the others. "The International Shark Attack File shows only four unprovoked attacks from Caribbean reef sharks in history. *Ever*. And no deaths."

"Well, technically … attacks on spearfishers are considered a provoked attack," Boone said.

"Oh…" Lucky said, looking back at his phone.

"So how many…?" Emily began, looking over Lucky's shoulder.

"Twenty-three. Still, not much."

"I've been working in this hospital for twenty years," the doctor said. "This is only the second bite I've treated. The other was on a fisherman trying to free one from a line. No diver has ever been bitten before."

"What about decompression sickness?" Boone asked. "The attack happened at about forty feet. I tried to come up in a controlled manner, but I admit I may have been a bit fuzzy at the end."

"I spoke to the technician down at the hyperbaric chamber in Fort Bay. I understand this young lady brought your computers to him?" Emily nodded. "He said neither of you were in the red and the ascent rates seemed reasonable. Neither computer locked you out, he said. As long as there are no DCS symptoms, you both should be fine. Still, pay attention to your body for a while."

As the doctor went back to Chad's room, Anika sat down with a sob, her eyes tearing up. "I shouldn't have let him do it."

"Anika, don't beat yourself up," Lucky said. "He's one of the best lionfish cullers on the island. It was just a freak accident. Hell, *I* woulda let him do it, if I'd been skippering."

Boone placed a gentle hand on Anika's shoulder. "He'll be fine, Anika."

"And *you* … You could've…"

"Hey, that was *my* decision. But if I'd taken the minute or two to suit up with a new tank, I wouldn't have been there in time. And that blackout was on me, too. I thought I had enough air, but I must've exerted myself more than I thought. And you got us back to port lickety-split with paramedics waiting. You saved Chad."

"And think of it this way, 'Nika," Emily said. "Now Chad's going to have a shark bite scar to show off to all the ladies. You've just upped his game!"

Anika managed a smile. "Is that a good thing?" she asked with a sniffle.

16

The following morning, Boone was down in Fort Bay, assisting Lucky with the preparations to bring the *Shoal 'Nuff* up the boat ramp and into storage in The Bottom. Emily was in the office with Anika, the Dutch girl finishing up the last of the cancellations and reschedulings while Emily pored through weather data.

"I'm telling you, Sophie is an excellent teacher," Anika was saying. "The self-defense tricks she's taught me have really boosted my confidence. Not like I need it here on Saba. There's probably less crime here than anywhere in the Caribbean. But it's nice to know if I need to defend myself, I'll know right away what to do. Come on. Join us!"

"Well…" Emily thought about it. In hindsight, she might have overreacted a bit when the green-eyed jealousy monster had come a-knockin'. And apparently Sophie was trying to mend fences, suggesting to Anika that she invite Emily along for their Sunday "lunch-and-lessons." And, truth to tell, watching Boone practice martial arts in Bonaire, Emily had found herself wishing she had some of that skill.

"Oh, bugger it, okay! I'm in."

"Wonderful!" Anika immediately began texting Sophie. "And if you enjoy that, maybe I can get you to join me and the Saba Lace Ladies … I like to do that before going over to Scout's for Tricia's Martini Night."

"Wait … "Saba Lace Ladies"? That sounds like some sort of burlesque dance group."

Anika giggled shyly. "No, no … Saba Lace is a unique kind of needlework. It used to be the main industry for the island, but there are only a few who practice it now. The ones who still know the art are trying to teach it to others. See?" She reached up and removed the scarf she had tied her hair back with, unfurling it and spreading it on the table. The drawn-thread stitches were incredibly intricate and delicate.

"It's beautiful! Did you make this?"

"Oh, no, I wish I had. I'm still learning. Grace made this for me. We all get together in the shop next to Sea Saba on Thursday afternoons. It's kind of like those quilting bees they have in America." She leaned forward. "And a good place to pick up juicy gossip."

"Count me in!"

Anika returned to her texting. "So, where is Miss Irma?" she asked as she typed. "Any change?"

"Winds are up a little, but still no watches or warnings. Fingers crossed, yeah?"

Out on the *Shoal 'Nuff,* Boone paused to take a drink of water. He had come to the boat the evening before to hose down the deck and get Chad's equipment together, putting everything into the shop. At the moment, he was stowing several items in the small bow hold, things that might blow free if left up top. Fenders, buoys, boat hooks, hoses—he secured them all below. When everything seemed clear, he got down on his hands and knees and looked all around. Bits of gear or trash frequently ended up under dive benches as the boat rolled and pitched, and sure enough he spotted something: one of Chad's chainmail gloves, crammed in a corner against the gunwale at the end of the starboard bench. He snaked a long arm under the bench and retrieved it, stuffing into one of the roomy thigh pockets on his cargo shorts.

"Think we're almost done here," Lucky said. "I'll put the covers on her once she's in The Bottom."

"What time will your friend be here with the trailer?" Boone asked.

"He said 'bout eleven. But you know 'Island Time'. That could mean after lunch."

A cheer went up from across the little harbor as the first of Sea Saba's boats left the main pier and headed out to sea on its run to Saint Martin. The other boat followed almost immediately, the remaining dive staff waving their farewells.

"How long will it take them to reach Saint Martin?" Boone asked.

"A couple hours, maybe a little more," Lucky replied.

A single boat remained at the main pier: a small, sleek Coast Guard vessel, its gray hull brightened by a diagonal yellow stripe along with the red, white, and blue of the Dutch flag. A new flash of color caught the corner of Boone's eye as a blue-and-orange striped police car rounded the bend from the road to The Bottom and drove past, pulling over near the Customs and Immigration office. Three men got out. The driver was a black policeman Boone didn't recognize, but the other two were Sid and his father. Sid saw Boone and waved, starting over to him. Captain Every remained at the car, chatting with the other policeman.

"Boone, I was hoping you'd be here," Sid began. "Your tip paid off. My father's headed to Statia right now to meet with the police over there. I know this is last minute, but … do you want to go?"

Boone blinked. "Isn't there a hurricane out there?"

"Not close enough to affect the crossing and Statia's only twenty miles away. Actually, the fact that Irma is coming means the Dutch need to juggle a few resources between islands. The Coast Guard dropped off a few Dutch marines here and they're taking some more over to Statia, so dad gets a free ride!"

"Okay … but why me?"

"Well, for one thing, when my father told the Statian police who it was that suggested we call them, they wanted to meet you." When Boone looked confused, Sid plowed on. "It's not everyday someone blows up a bunch of terrorists. Everyone over there knows about it."

"So I'll send over some autographs," Boone said.

"Okay, that's not the main reason. Look, I haven't known you long but it's clear to me you have good instincts. I was talking about it this morning to Sophie and she's the one who said I should twist your arm and ask you. Honestly, I just want your intuition over there with my father."

"You're not going?"

"No, I need to stay here and help with storm prep. And keep canvassing for the missing couple."

Boone looked to Lucky. "Well, boss?"

"Like I said, we're about done. Fine by me, if it's fine with your *other* boss."

Boone laughed, turning back to Sid. "Yeah, I'm afraid I don't get the final say. Lemme check with Emily."

———◆•◆———

"Am I invited?" Emily asked, after Boone explained Sid's request. She rocked in Lucky's desk chair. Boone sat on the inside edge of the desk beside her.

"Uh … probably? I can ask. Hell, I can make it a requirement."

"Actually, I have plans." Emily said, leaning back in the desk chair, tucking her hands behind her head. Boone felt a stirring at what that movement did to the light green tank top she was wearing. As was often the case, Emily saw it in his eyes. She swiveled the chair back and forth in quarter circles. "What, see something you like?"

"Every minute of every day," Boone said, meaning every word.

Emily halted her chair wobbles. "Good answer, Mr. Fischer." She simply looked at him for a moment. Then: "You really scared me yesterday."

"I know. I'm sorry."

Emily shot out of the chair and planted a deep kiss on Boone's lips, gripping the back of his hair. After a moment she withdrew. "It was very selfish of you to wake up before I had a chance to give you mouth-to-mouth, so I think I was owed that."

"I would've kept my eyes closed longer and pretended, had I known."

She broke off and plopped back into the seat. "As much as I'd love to dash across the sea with a boatful of men in uniform, I have a date."

"You do, do you?"

"What, you think you have a monopoly on my affections? I'm going out with Sophie."

Boone hadn't expected *that*. "Really?"

"First we're doing lunch. Then Sophie's going to teach me self-defense. Anika's coming too! Just so you know, it *might* turn into a threesome. Depends on if there's drinks with lunch and how much rolling around on the ground we do."

Boone laughed and slid from the desk, planting a long kiss of his own on Emily's lips. Withdrawing, he held her eyes. "You girls have fun. And use protection."

Emily's eyes went wide, her mouth open in amused shock. "Boone!"

"What? I meant gym mats, knee pads, mouth guards! Get your mind out of the gutter, Em." He winked and headed for the exit before she could smack him.

17

"There she is, The Golden Rock," Captain Every said as the Dutch Caribbean Coast Guard cutter *Puma* sliced through the indigo waters between Saba and Statia. They were standing on the upper deck alongside the pilot house, enjoying the morning sun.

Ahead, the island of Sint Eustatius came into sharper focus. It was shaped like a teardrop, the smaller, northern end consisting of rocky hills and scrub, uninhabited except for a surprisingly large expanse of white oil tanks. Beyond lay a relatively flat saddle of land where most of the population lived. Far to the south, the massive stratovolcano named The Quill rose above all, its flanks an emerald green. Unlike Mount Scenery on Saba, which had a mountainy look, The Quill was clearly a volcano, its squat, cone-shaped mass topped by a clearly-defined crater.

"*Golden* Rock? Um … okay." They were coming at it from the northwest, so the northern tip was most prominent. The predominant color Boone saw there was brown.

"It's hard to believe, but there was a time when Sint Eustatius was one of the biggest trading hubs in the Caribbean."

"Really?" Boone had landed at the little airport there on his way to Saba and the island had seemed far less developed than Bonaire or Curaçao.

"I know, it doesn't look like much, but it had a good harbor and, more importantly, no customs duties. Most of the British, French, and Spanish ports had monopolistic trade with substantial tariffs in place. Here, traders bringing in goods could make a tidy profit. Some days, there were over 200 ships in the harbor."

"You moonlight as a history professor when you're not policing?"

Captain Every smiled under his mustache. "Bit of a hobby."

As the cutter neared Statia, they encountered a dense yellow slick of sargassum, but the bow of the *Puma* parted the floating seaweed with ease. Closer to the island, the scale of the oil tanks in the hills came into sharper focus, dominating the northern part of Sint Eustatius. An extremely long jetty extended from shore into deep water. Boone estimated its length at over half a mile. A large oil tanker was alongside the jetty and nearby, two other tankers waited at anchor.

"When I was a boy, there was nothing over here. Now, after a major oil shipment company moved in, it's one of the largest oil transshipment storage facilities in the Western Hemisphere."

"On that tiny island?"

"Believe me, not everyone is happy about it. My Statian friends say it's definitely brought jobs to the island, but it's also brought massive amounts of tanker traffic. And that means damage to the reefs from anchors, pollution ... oil spills. Normally, there would be a lot more tankers here, but with the storm coming, this is probably the last of them for a while."

South of the oil terminal, the inhabited part of the island came into view. Three smaller boats were anchored in the shallows and Boone could make out several small docks in the vicinity of the few buildings that stood along the shore. To the south was a larger pier inside a breakwater and an area for offloading cargo. Above the waterfront, a cliff ran along the middle of the island and Boone could see numerous buildings up top, including the low walls of a fortress on an outcrop.

"Looks like the pier is full up," Boone noted.

Captain Every nodded. "Likely everyone is preparing to secure their boats over here too." He pointed toward a short pier next to a tiny building. "See that framework on that pier? It's a boat lift. That will probably be getting some heavy use in the next few days. The little building next to it, the one with the red trim, that's Golden Rock Dive Center." Boone could feel the engines on the cutter slow to an idle as a young Dutch sailor joined them on the pilot house deck. "Gentlemen, we'll be anchoring here. If you'll join us aft at the stern ramp, we'll be sending a launch ashore with the contingent of marines."

Heading aft, Boone came up short as he looked across the cutter's stern to the north. Under the blue skies, the island of Saba was visible in the distance, the distinctive shape of the island on display with a single cloud nestled on the tip of Mount Scenery, obscuring the summit from sight. "Wow. That's a view."

"Home, sweet home," the captain remarked. "And if we were out a bit from the bay, you'd have a great view of Saint Kitts. She's only about eight miles to the southeast."

Ten minutes after the cutter dropped anchor, Boone, Captain Every, and four Royal Dutch Marines were aboard a rigid inflatable boat, or RIB, and on their way to the smaller pier. As they neared the shore, a shadow passed overhead. Boone looked up as a Magnificent Frigatebird glided by, its throat sporting an impressive red neck pouch. After the RIB tied up, the marines disembarked first, remaining on the pier to wait for another four who were still aboard the cutter. Boone and Captain Every walked toward the Golden Rock Dive Center, heading for the road.

"Clark! You be wanting a ride, or are you gonna climb up the side of the cliff like the Saban mountain goat y'are?"

The voice came from the shaded area at the front of the dive shop. A police officer sat there, polishing off the last of a sandwich. Dark-skinned and portly, he had a smattering of freckles on his plump cheeks. Smiling, he rose to greet them, tossing his wrapper into a nearby trash can.

"Surprised to see you out of the air co, Axel," Captain Clark Every said with a grin, shaking the man's hand.

The policeman caught Boone's puzzled expression. "This silly Saban means air conditioning. Too lazy to say all the syllables. It's a bit hotter over here. We don't get to live a mile in the air."

"Boone, this is Major Axel Jones, the police chief for Sint Eustatius. Axel, this is Boone Fischer."

"So *you're* the submarine slayer!" Major Jones grabbed Boone's hand and shook it vigorously. "Very pleased to meet you. Do you know, I was up at the oil terminal that day and we heard the explosion. You must tell me all about it! But first—" he gestured to his police car in front of the shop, sporting the same blue-and-orange stripes as the ones on Saba "—let's get up to Oranjestad. Clark is right, I do like my air co."

As they drove along the waterside road, Boone noted the ruins of old warehouses overgrown with vines. Passing under the fortress he'd seen from aboard the cutter, he asked "What is that fort up there on the outcrop?"

"That's Fort Oranje. You're American, right?"

Boone looked puzzled for a moment. "Yeah, grew up in Tennessee. My dad was Dutch. American mom. Why do you ask?"

"Some fun history for you. That fort fired the very first salute to the American flag."

"Really?"

"If it weren't for Statia, you might still be British. We were a major supplier of arms and gunpowder to the colonies during the American Revolution. And your Benjamin Franklin? He had all his European correspondence routed through here."

"So ... what Americans did the fort salute?"

"A rebel brig, the *Andrew Doria*. She'd been busy capturing British ships in the Atlantic but was ordered here to pick up a load of munitions. She fired a thirteen-gun salute, one for each colony, and the governor ordered an eleven-gun reply."

"Why eleven?"

"International custom was to fire two guns less than the visiting ship, when saluting a sovereign flag."

Captain Every got a sly look on his face. "The story *I* heard was that the governor didn't recognize the flag and fired the salute just to be on the safe side."

"Just like a Saban, to try to steal Statia's thunder," the major said, waggling his finger at Captain Every. "You don't know beef from bull's foot. Bunch of pirates," he muttered with good humor.

◆•◆

"So ... Krav Maga ... what exactly does that mean?" Emily asked, taking a long pull on the disposable straw in her mango smoothie. Saba Snack had run out of fresh soursop and she'd had to make do with a different delicious fruit. The three women had finished their lunch of quesadillas and were relaxing in the patio area.

"It's Hebrew for 'contact combat.' The Israeli Defense Force teaches it and Krav has become popular with many militaries around the world." Sophie stretched her long legs to the side of their table.

They just go on for days, don't they? Emily thought. "Go on," she said aloud.

"Best way I can sum it up: strike fast, strike hard, strike repeatedly. Whatever works best, that's what you do."

"So … do I get to jump through the air with my leg out, all Bruce Lee?" Emily asked.

Anika laughed and Sophie smiled. "If it works for you, sure … but unless you *are* Bruce Lee, I wouldn't recommend it. Actually, even if you were. You want to stay grounded. And you want to play to your assets."

Emily eyed Sophie's long, sculpted legs. "Speaking of assets, you seem built for kicking."

Sophie waved the compliment away. "How tall are you, Emily?"

"Four-eleven. But after a massage I can fake a five."

Sophie laughed. "Well, you're going to need to make your size your strength. Sometimes the best tactic is to strike low."

"What, kick 'em in the goolies?"

"If that means 'balls', then yes. Fastest way to end a fight. But I'll teach you some moves that aren't so crass. For instance, if I grab you from behind, what would you do?"

"Besides scream for help?"

"I know you mean that as a joke, but that is *exactly* what you would do … it's what *I* would do. But besides that?"

"Stomp on the instep," Anika suggested. "One of the first things Sophie showed me."

"It only takes four and a half pounds to break the tarsal bones in the foot," Sophie instructed. "The sudden pain is likely to loosen your opponent's grip and if you can break free and run, they're not going to be able to keep up with a smashed foot."

Emily nodded. "Right-o, very sensible. But can you teach me some cool, flashy stuff too? Nut punches and foot stomps are all well and good, but…"

"Don't worry, Emily," Anika said. "Sophie will show you some great moves. She's just covering the basics."

"Remember, whatever ends the fight fast, that's what you want to do." Sophie said. "But yes, I can show you all sorts of cool stuff. Don't you worry."

"So, where do we train?"

"I use a space over in the school in Saint John's. It's Sunday, so we can head over any time you like."

"Well, I don't want to pound my smoothie or I'll succumb to brain freeze. Let's chill for a bit, yeah?"

Anika touched her arm. "Emily, I can take you back to your place after we train, so Sophie won't have to backtrack. Where are you staying again?"

"Boone has secured suitable accommodations in the English Quarter," Emily said, softening her rough South London dialect into a faux-posh accent before dropping it and resuming in her normal voice. "Actually, the view is ace! It's a little cottage on an outcrop, just on the edge of Windwardside. Has a cute name. Hummingbird Haven. There's almost always a hummingbird or two out back. One day, there were—"

"Hey! Can I help you?"

The sudden aggression in Sophie's voice jarred Emily from her hummingbird reminiscence. She turned to see where Sophie was glaring. A tall man in gray coveralls and a ball cap was mumbling an apology, turning away and crossing the road before vanishing into the Big Rock Supermarket across the street. Emily noticed he had blond hair beneath his cap but what really drew her eyes were numerous blotches and streaks of yellow on the coveralls. *Maybe a painter,* she thought. *Except, that doesn't look like paint.*

"Creep," Sophie muttered.

"What was that all about?" Emily asked.

"That man was staring at us," Anika said.

"He was staring at Emily," Sophie amended.

Emily looked toward the door of the supermarket, then polished off her smoothie. "Brain freeze be damned, I suddenly have the urge to learn some Krav Maga."

Fool! You have been so careful and now you stand in the middle of the street, staring like a child. You have what you need!

But she was perfect... *perfect.*

Perfection is not necessary. Only obedience. Only success. You were provided with the opportunity and you seized it. The choice has been made.

But, she ... I still have three days. Perhaps—

This is your vanity. This is your own desire speaking. Your own lust.

No, you misunderstand. This one is so small, and I have to carry—

Silence! We have made you strong, have we not?

Yes. Yes, you have. And each time, I grow stronger still.

Then return to the one who was Chosen and await the moment.

"Sir? Sir? Did you need something else?"

The Servant blinked. He was standing in front of the cash register, a basket of groceries in one hand and a can of lentil soup in the other. The cashier, a middle-aged woman with horn-rimmed glasses, peered at him nervously.

"Sir? Are you all right?"

The Servant instantly lit up a smile on his handsome face. "Yes. Forgive me. I thought I'd forgotten something. Um, yes, I do need something else. Ring up a case of water bottles, too. I'll grab them on the way out."

While the cashier rang up the order, the Servant stepped to the glass doors and looked across the street. The women were gone.

18

"Her name is Imke De Wit. Dutch national." Major Jones was reading from an open file folder on the desk in his tiny office inside the police station in Oranjestad. Being the only town on the island, it was the capital of Sint Eustatius. "She was here for a summer abroad, studying orchids in the crater of The Quill for her university degree." He looked up and gestured vaguely to his left, toward the south. "We have sixteen endangered species of orchid up there, and nine of them only occur on The Quill." He looked back down to the report. "She was last seen on the evening of August 5, leaving a bar near Fort Oranje. Miss De Wit's roommate reported that she did not return home that night."

"Did anyone see her leave the bar?" Captain Every asked.

"Yes. The bartender said she left the bar alone, around eleven."

"Was she with anyone at the bar?"

"The bartender said she was with two friends, both women, who left earlier. He also said a man bought her a drink, but he left earlier too."

"What did he look like?" Boone asked.

Major Jones flipped a page in the report. "White male. Tall, over six feet. Blond hair."

Boone sat up straighter. "Did the bartender recognize him?"

"The bartender is a longtime local and he didn't know the man. With the oil terminal, we get many workers and ships' crews from all over, even more than the tourists. He thought he was American, though. But the man only spoke when he ordered the drink, so the bartender couldn't be sure."

Captain Every made a few notes in a pad. "She hasn't contacted family, I assume? No cell phone use?"

"Nothing. The phone appears to be off. And WinAir says no one matching her description has left the island, according to their records."

"Well, it's possible she left by boat," the captain suggested.

"Have you searched The Quill?" Boone blurted out.

"Well, no … she wouldn't have gone up there at night. Only ones who do that are locals, if they're hunting soldiers."

"Soldiers?"

"Big, purple land crabs," Captain Every interjected. "We have them on Saba. Lollipop's up in Saint John's serves them sometimes."

"There was no crab hunt that night," Major Jones continued. "I checked. Also, all her equipment and orchid notes were in her apartment." The major turned to Captain Every. "Your missing couple … anything new?"

"No, nothing yet. Preparations for Hurricane Irma have been taking most of our resources."

"Yes, here too." The major leaned back in his chair to look at the wall clock behind his head. "We should be getting an update on the track soon. Hopefully she'll steer north." He grabbed a yellow stress ball from a corner of his desk and squeezed it repeatedly. "We're hoping Miss De Wit will show up, but it's been a month."

"Major," came a voice from the door. "I couldn't help overhear you talking about our missing persons case." A young, black policewoman poked her head in. "Sorry to interrupt."

"That's all right. Constable Amber Holmes, this is Boone Fischer. And you know this old goat."

The constable smiled. "Hello, Captain Every."

"Good to see you, Amber. Constable, eh? You're moving up."

Major Jones tossed the stress ball in an arc and began crushing it in his other hand. "Constable, did you have something to add, or did you just pop by to let me know you've been eavesdropping?"

"Well, sir … with our missing girl, and now these two on Saba, I was thinking I'd heard of another disappearance from my sister over on Saint Kitts. I called her and sure enough, there was a girl who went missing the beginning of July."

The stress ball received a final epic squeeze before dropping to the desk. "Really?"

"One every month…" Boone said to himself.

"Huh," the major muttered, thinking. "Let me call over to Kitts and see what information they have to share. It might take a while, so let's do this: go grab an early bite, and I'll come join you when I've spoken with them."

Captain Every stood. "Sounds like a plan. If you don't mind, I think we'll head over to the Kings Well. I haven't seen Win and Laura in ages and Win makes the best wiener schnitzel." He turned to Boone. "Win is German. Makes for a nice change from the usual Caribbean food."

Boone and Captain Every stepped outside and the captain lit up a cigarette. "Horrible habit, I know. Thank goodness Sid hasn't picked it up." He blew a rush of smoke and looked to the south, where the massive, cone-shaped Quill loomed over the landscape. "You know, our Mount Scenery is a thousand feet taller, but we live *on* it. Here, everyone lives on this flat plain and looks up at that. Makes The Quill seem so much larger."

"Is it active?"

"No, no … dormant. I hiked it once. The Quill has a large crater and inside is a thick, tropical rainforest. I climbed down there, holding a rope for safety. There were some trees that looked like they were from an alien world, gnarly roots twisting and twining like a kraken's tentacles."

"And orchids? De Wit was studying orchids, right?"

"Actually, most of the orchids are at the higher elevations, around the rim." He took another drag off the cigarette.

Boone looked back at the building with its bright blue walls and red roof, the Dutch word for police, *Politie*, over the door, the Dutch and Statian flags flying to the right of the entrance. "Sometimes, it's easy to forget these islands are Dutch. Everyone speaks English. Everyone uses the U.S. dollar."

"True," the captain mused. "But the same could be said for a lot of Caribbean islands."

A flash of color in the sky drew Boone's eye. "Is that…? No, I'm seeing things." A large red bird with flashes of blue and yellow flew overhead, heading toward the west.

Captain Every laughed. "You're not imagining it. That's a scarlet macaw."

"But those aren't indigenous up here. Are they?"

"They're indigenous to the Kings Well. You'll probably see them. Laura keeps a few and a couple of them are allowed to fly around. I had breakfast with them once, on the little balcony they have on the cliffside. I didn't share my eggs with one of them fast enough and he grabbed my salt shaker in his beak and dropped it off the cliff."

The glass doors behind them opened and Constable Holmes came out. "Oh, good, I caught you. The Major thought you'd want to know. It's official: Statia and Saba are now under a hurricane watch."

———— ◆ • ◆ ————

An hour later, Boone and Captain Every were ensconced at the bar in the Kings Well. The owners had given Boone a quick tour and he loved the old-world charm of the place, its grounds filled with tropical foliage and numerous iguanas, macaws, and two enormous Great Danes, Sam and Sasha. Several cats prowled about as well. Win Piechutzki was busy preparing his famous *jäger schnitzel*. He didn't have any veal for the "wiener" schnitzel, so this version was breaded pork chops, pounded flat and slathered with a brown mushroom gravy, served over egg noodles. Living in the islands, Boone tended to gravitate toward fresh seafood, but the description of this German dish had him salivating.

"Boone Fischer? You wanted another blue bead so much you come over already?"

Standing at the entrance to the dining room, Reynaldo held an industrial bucket in one hand. He wore a shorty wetsuit, still damp, so battered and worn that its age was likely in the decades. Flipping up the hinged end of the bar, he set the bucket just inside.

"Win, I got your conch." Win waved an acknowledgement and Reynaldo helped himself to a Presidente beer from the under-bar fridge and joined Boone at the bar, nodding to Captain Every. "Captain."

"Reynaldo," the captain replied, warily. "Wait a minute…" He looked at Boone. "He's the Statian who told you about the missing girl, isn't he?"

"Uh…"

"What were you doing in Saba, Rey?" Captain Every asked.

"Transiting, a' course. On my way to Saint Martin. Happen to run into Boone here on da way."

"Saba's pretty far out of the way for a run to Saint Martin, Rey."

"Hey, you hear we're on a hurricane watch?" Boone interjected to change the subject. "You going to bring your boat in? Maybe use that boat lift on the pier we came in on?"

"What, dat metal sculpture on Ro Ro pier? Dat ain't work in years. No, I'll take her south to Nevis in da morn. Got a friend with space at a dock. You two come in on dat cutter, uh?"

"Yes," Every replied. "We'll be heading back to it shortly after Major Jones joins us."

"You must be good swimmers, den."

"What do you mean?"

"She was weighin' anchor when I was deshellin' the conch down on da pier."

"What?" Captain Every frantically dug his cell phone out of a pocket. "Cack, no service! Win, what's the Wi-Fi password?" The old German tapped a laminated card on the bar and went back to his schnitzel. Punching it into his phone, the captain tapped the screen. "Mudda…" He looked up. "They had to leave after the official hurricane watch was declared. Reynaldo, can you take us across?"

Reynaldo chupsed, sucking his teeth. "Now Captain, dat's a tall order for me. My friend is expecting me tomorrow and I don't want to lose dat slip."

"You worrying about the cutter leaving you high and dry?" Major Jones laughed as he ambled into the dining area, sporting a messenger bag. "You know, if you were a Statian, you would have thought to have checked in with them." He leaned in toward Boone, speaking in a conspiratorial whisper. "It's the altitude. Sabans don't get enough oxygen to the brain."

"We don't need as much, since we're in better shape." Captain Every poked the major in his ample belly.

"Ooh nelly, going personal, are you? Don't get me started on that mustache, you old walrus." He clapped a friendly hand on the Saban's shoulder. "Don't you worry. The cutter called me, said they couldn't reach you. I pulled some strings and got you seats on a WinAir flight for Saint Martin in the morning. They'll swing by Saba and drop you off. I'm sure Win and Laura can put you up for the night."

"Ja, ja, no problem," came from the vicinity of the sizzling schnitzel.

"Rey, I have some sensitive police business to discuss..." the major began.

"And I have some udda stops to make," the old Statian said. "Boone, before you go to bed, drop by Smoke Alley for a beer."

"They're open on a Sunday?" Major Jones asked.

Reynaldo shrugged. "They're open when they're open. I ran into the owner and he said he'd be there."

"Where is it?" Boone asked.

Reynaldo stepped onto the tiny balcony that jutted from the dining area and pointed down along the cliff. "Right dere. Just take da road down around da bend and follow da music."

After taking payment for the conch, Reynaldo left and the three adjourned to one of the three plastic patio tables on the balcony.

Major Jones withdrew De Wit's file from the messenger bag as well as a new folder, unmarked and thin. He flipped it open.

"So, our friends on Saint Kitts emailed me what they had. Turns out it's no longer a missing persons case. It's a murder."

"Sha!" Captain Every cursed.

"Who was she?" Boone asked quietly.

"Luna Alvarez. Dominican girl, worked as a waitress in Basse-terre."

"Anyone arrested for the crime?" Every asked.

"Not as yet."

"Where did they find her?"

Major Jones shifted in his chair, looking uncomfortable. "The chief of police called me back himself. Asked that I keep the specifics confidential."

"Of course," the captain responded, and Boone nodded his assent.

The major cleared his throat. "Her body was found on July 10, near the summit of Mount Liamuiga, a little ways off the trail. A pair of hikers found her."

"They think she was on a hike with the killer?" Captain Every asked.

"Possible. It makes sense—the hike up there is very strenuous. Rough trails. But no one knows for sure. Her restaurant said she just didn't show up for work. No leads."

"How did she…?" Boone began, trailing off.

Major Jones sighed and looked out at the water. The sun was nearing the horizon and backlit a nearby tanker. "She was nearly decapitated. They think a machete was used. The cut was so deep, the spinal cord was severed."

"Sha!" Captain Every rasped. "Bad-minded people in this world…"

"Could I see that?" Boone asked, indicating the folder. The major spun it around for him. Boone scanned the pages but settled on a single page devoted to the woman herself. She was young, objectively beautiful, and…

"Wait, could I see your file, too?" Boone asked quickly.

Jones grumbled something about confidential information but handed it over when Captain Every gave a subtle nod. Boone located the part of the report that focused on the particulars of the missing Imke De Wit. He scanned the information below her smiling photo. Also young. And also …

He looked up. "Captain, the missing couple on Saba, how tall was the girl?"

"Uh … I don't recall offhand. One moment." He opened a notepad app on his phone and scanned a file. Five-foot-four, a hundred-thirty-five pounds. Why?"

"It's probably nothing … I just noticed that *these* two women," he tapped the files in front of him, "were both five feet tall, petite, and on the youngish side." He looked down at the Saint Kitts printouts and chewed his lip. "This … Mount Liamuiga. Is it a volcano?"

"Yes," Captain Every said. "Big stratovolcano, almost a thousand feet taller than Saba's."

Boone looked down at Imke De Wit's picture. "Major Jones, I really think you should search The Quill."

Later that evening, Boone strolled downhill toward the sounds of calypso. The Smoke Alley Bar and Grill stood on a gravelly patch at the rocky shore alongside a black sand beach. The rustic open-air structure looked like it had seen better days and it wasn't exactly hopping, but there were seven or eight patrons, and a DJ attended to the music with great relish. Boone spied Reynaldo right away and the wiry old Statian waved him over. "You came," he said, motioning to the bartender for a Presidente for Boone.

"I somehow got the feeling that the invitation was more than a casual suggestion."

"Where's your pretty little friend?"

"She's holding down the fort over in Saba."

"Before I forget, you got a phone for over dere? Gimme da number."

Boone found the number and gave it to Reynaldo. The music changed to a faster beat and Boone glanced over at the DJ.

"You're in luck," Reynaldo said. "Private is in rare form. Putting in some of his own songs, too."

"Private?"

"It's his name, The Artist Private. Leoncio was deejaying on the radio back in da day and people called in wanting to know who it was. Him was working at da fire department at da time and didn't want to give his name … so dey said 'It's Private.' And da name stuck."

Boone popped the cap on his beer and took a swig. "He's good."

"Good performer too, back in da day. And Mighty Fat, also. Him a baker by day. Makes da johnnycakes for Statia."

"I'm sure I'll be back. And I promise I'll bring Emily next time. So, what did you want to see me about?"

"I was t'inking about dat boat you were on when you kill da submarine."

"The *Wavy Davey?*"

Reynaldo nodded. "You know she was over here?"

"No. When?"

"Beginning of da month, not long after dat Dutch girl go missing. They were moored in da bay for a day, den came to the pier the night before dey leff for Saba. Dem boys smugglers. I recognize one of dem. German man. He no good."

"Them … there were two?"

"Ya, mon. Two smugglers. But when dey left, dere was three."

Boone frowned. "Another smuggler joined them?"

"I don't think dis boy was a smuggler. I was on my boat at Ro Ro pier. Him come to me few hours before dawn, lookin' all sweaty. Ask me to take him to Saba. Flashed a lot of American dollars."

"But you didn't take him."

"No, mon. Him give off a bad vibe. I told him da boat was broke. He thank me nice enough but de thank you don't reach his eyes. I watch him go over to the main pier where I see him talk to da German. Not long after, the *Wavy Davey* leave with all three of them aboard, heading for Saba."

"When was this, exactly?"

"I remember dere was a full moon that night, so early da next morning."

"What did the man look like?" Boone asked.

"Him was almost as tall as you. White boy, blond hair, big muscles." Reynaldo reached across and touched the blue bead at Boone's throat. "And he have one of dese."

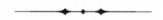

The Servant tossed the package containing the passport forgeries on the floor beside his backpack. Wink had been true to his word and the final product was professionally done. Gunter would be pleased, and the money he handed over would allow the Servant to continue his calling for the foreseeable future.

"You should feel pride, you know," the Servant said in the sickly glow of the LED lantern. "It is a high honor to be Chosen."

The prisoner made no reply, her eyes reflecting the light. If fear was behind those eyes it was dulled by a haze of fatigue and repeated doses of sedatives.

"This ball of rock and water and gas that we live on? She is a living, breathing creature." He sat on the earthen floor of the cellar, kneading his fingers in the soil. "Well ... I say 'she', but of course the Earth doesn't have a gender. But using 'it' just seems ... disrespectful. Not that she gives a shit what some little speck of flesh calls her."

The Servant laughed, a mirthless rattle of sound. He reached up to his throat, his fingers finding the little sphere of pumice stone from Montserrat. The feel of the tiny holes on its surface was soothing as he rolled it between the pads of his fingertips. He missed the smooth glass surfaces of the Statian bead, but this volcano-borne trophy was his favorite.

"She *lives*, as surely as you or I. Methane, sulphur dioxide, all the gases that she belches forth? Her breath. The tectonic plates that grind together, shaking the ground ... her muscles, flexing and contracting. The molten rock that oozes through the magma chambers of the earth ... her blood, flowing through subterranean arteries, interconnecting her many, many hearts. At this very moment we are above one such heart. She slumbers now ... but it is time for her to awaken. We humans...we are insignificant flecks of organic matter on the surface of her skin. Like mites. Or bacteria. Polluting her oceans. Her air. Tearing into her flesh for coal, or oil, or gold ... or sulphur, as they did here on this island.

We have mistreated her. Disrespected her. *Sickened* her. But she has ways to counter the disease.

"Take a pyroclastic flow: hot ash, nearly 2,000 degrees Fahrenheit, roaring down on a sleeping town at hundreds of miles per hour, burning, melting, smothering everything in its path. Clouds of ash so big they generate their own lightning! You have no *idea* of the power she possesses. She just needs a little help. A little nudge. And that's where *you* come in."

He looked at the girl, watching for a response. There was none. She stared dully at him, and the Servant felt a burst of anger.

"Are you *listening* to what I'm telling you? Why is it *none* of you ever understand?" He felt the rough surface of the pumice rolling across his fingertips as his mind drifted back in time to that fateful summer mission trip on Montserrat. The time where he had received his *true* calling.

Lucy. She had been so beautiful, his golden-haired angel, his petite flower, and he had *lusted* for her there in the ash-strewn remains of Plymouth. After so many fumbling and fruitless attempts at romance with women who had scorned his advances, here had been the perfect woman. He had met her at orientation for the trip and she had taken his breath away. He had found himself unable to talk to her that day, but then Fate had intervened, placing them *together* on the flight from the States. Out of all the seats she could have been in, it was the one next to his. And what's more, she had fallen asleep against his shoulder. Her hair had smelled of lavender—he remembered that scent so distinctly, so sharply. After they landed in nearby Antigua, Lucy had awakened with a bright smile, teasing him about having used his muscles for a pillow. She had traced a fingernail against his biceps, the sensation sending tremors throughout his body. He'd only recently begun a weight-lifting regimen and had a mere fraction of the strength he now possessed, but his muscles were well-defined and it was clear that she ... *liked* them. Liked *him*.

It seemed like destiny. Three days into the mission trip, after a long day of work they snatched a night, enjoying each other's kisses and clumsy fumblings. But when the time came for more ... things changed. It had not gone well. And she had laughed. She'd apologized and gifted him with a gentle kiss before departing, leaving him alone with his thoughts. And that night ... some of the thoughts ... *some* of them were not his own.

In the early part of the mission trip, the man who would become the Servant had become fascinated with the devastation on Monserrat caused by the volcanic eruption, and after that night, new beliefs bloomed. The next day he'd found Lucy and suggested a hike into the outskirts of the ash-strewn ruins of the former capital, now abandoned. Perhaps feeling guilty for the previous night, she'd obliged, despite the area being restricted.

He was sure that once she heard what he had to say, she would realize he was worthy of her affections. He wanted to share everything with her ... but just as the night before had ended in laughter, so too did this latest effort. When he'd attempted to explain his newfound knowledge of geomantic mysteries, she had openly mocked him. Called him ... *insane*. So he'd killed her. And some of the arousal that had been absent the night before arose in him then. A scorched machete he'd found in the ruins of an ash-buried cottage had provided the means, after he'd replaced its incinerated handle with a generous helping of duct tape. But though the execution was satisfying, it had been to no purpose—he hadn't done it *properly*. The still-active Soufrière Hills volcano had been too far away. It was only after, as he buried her body under the thickly packed ash of the pyroclastic flow, that he realized what a wasted opportunity it had been. The voices concurred: if he had timed it more precisely, at the correct location, he would have been of greater service. From time to time, the Earth required a sacrifice.

The Aztecs knew this. And the Mayans. The Incas, too. For the Incan Empire, Viracocha was both creator god and volcano god, and sacrifices were made to him. Mummified remains of young girls had been found on the upper slopes of both Mount Amato and Mount Llullaillaco, massive stratovolcanoes in the Andes. In what is now Mexico, the volcanoes Popocatepetl and Iztaccihuatl were personified by the Aztecs, deified with effigies. The Servant didn't believe in volcano gods per se, but he was convinced that a portion of the Earth's consciousness could be focused at the surface, the best focal point being a volcano, a "mouthpiece" to the Earth. And the voices he heard—true, they were probably his own thoughts, in part—but he was certain those thoughts manifested because of communications he was receiving. Maybe from vibrations in the ground? He wasn't sure. In Sint Eustatius, up on The Quill under the full moon, he could *swear* he had actually seen a manifestation of the Earth, looking a bit like Lucy, reaching out to him in gratitude. Thanking him for the sacrifice. But it had not been enough. The Great Awakening had not occurred.

"But *this* time will be different," the Servant spoke softly into the damp cellar air. A powerful hurricane, another form of the Earth's breath, was on its way, scheduled to hit this stratovolcano during the full moon, the time of peak fertility. "This time ... *your* blood will bring *her* blood and breath to the surface."

This time ... he saw the fear in those eyes.

19

Early the next morning, after a breakfast of eggs with the scarlet macaws, Boone and Captain Every were taken to the airport by Major Jones. Boone informed the major of what he'd learned from Rey, and Jones said he'd go get a full recounting from him. Arriving at the tiny Roosevelt Airport, they waited with a group of passengers at the tiny yellow-and-green airport terminal, though the word "terminal" was generous. After a quarter hour, a familiar rumble met their ears and a blue-and-white WinAir plane came into view, a little Twin Otter. Capable of Short Take-off and Landing, known as STOL, it was one of the few commercial aircraft able to land on Saba and the most common model used in the Northern Leewards. It landed effortlessly, the Statian runway being much longer than Saba's short airstrip. Several passengers exited and after luggage was unloaded, the plane was filled to capacity and swiftly returned to the skies.

Less than fifteen minutes later, Saba appeared in the cockpit window, as the Twin Otter approached Saba from the southwest.

"You're coming in from the south?" Captain Every asked, leaning into the aisle near the cockpit. He had to shout to be heard over the roar of the twin piston engines.

"Winds favor it today, and we're going on to Saint Martin so … yes," the co-pilot said. "No problem. We do it this way every once in a while."

"A first for me," the captain said, settling back into his seat and tightening his seat belt as the Twin Otter swept by the steep cliffs of Saba and dropped down onto the 400-meter runway of Juancho E. Yrausquin airport.

After exiting the terminal, they found Sophie waiting alongside a yellow firetruck, wearing a navy-blue uniform shirt and dark slacks. She waved and started toward them. "Welcome back! Sid's on his way." She pointed up the slope towards Hell's Gate. There, on the lengthy stretch of switchbacks, a police car was slowly slaloming its way down the winding road. "Emily is helping Lucky board up the shop. I guess you heard the latest."

"Yes," Captain Every said. "Hurricane watch."

"No, they just upgraded it. The entire Northern Leewards are now under a hurricane warning."

Boone noticed the members of the fire department were busy securing their equipment. Airport workers, too, were scurrying about. A hurricane watch had just meant that hurricane force winds were *possible*; a warning meant it was now likely. Sid's patrol car pulled up and his father headed straight for it. Boone lingered with Sophie. "How'd the training session go?"

Sophie smiled slyly. "Emily may not be big, but she's got some muscles on her! She's also a quick learner. I'm sure she'll tell you all about it. I better get back to work."

Boone joined Sid and his father and the three drove up The Road, heading for Windwardside. Sid ran through the preparations for the storm, nearly finishing by the time they descended toward The Bottom and the police station. "There'll be one more flight this afternoon—then the airport will shut down. Also, we've got some more Royal Dutch Marines on the way. We'll be putting them up at Child's Focus."

"And will we have a curfew in place?" his father asked.

"Yes. The governor signed off on it. Ten p.m. tomorrow night," Sid replied as they pulled up to the police station.

"Good. Go ahead and run Boone down to Fort Bay, then head up to the Windwardside annex to coordinate up there."

"Yes, sir."

Minutes later, Sid dropped Boone off at the harbor. The piers were completely empty of boats and most of the buildings along the little stretch of road were shuttered. Lucky and Emily were out front, hammering a length of plywood into place across one of the windows.

Emily's face lit up when Boone approached the shop. "About time!" She handed him her hammer. "I was afraid you were going to be stuck over there." She leaned in and gave him a gentle kiss below his ear. "Missed you," she whispered.

"You too," he replied softly, before hefting the hammer and assisting Lucky.

"Most of the buildings on Saba have proper shutters," Lucky said, hammering away, "but this old shop is gonna need a little extra help."

"Irma's up to a Category 4," Emily said. "Winds 130 last time I checked."

"You get your boat stored?" Boone asked Lucky.

"Yep, she's up in The Bottom on my buddy's lot. The village is in a kind of bowl surrounded by hills, so she should be protected from the wind."

Boone wasn't entirely sure that would be the case, since the terrain might actually funnel or focus the winds, but it would certainly be safer up there than down here in Fort Bay.

"So, did you and Sid's dad find out anything?" Emily asked.

As they hammered the last of the plywood into place, Boone gave her a quick summary, glossing over some of the more gruesome details. He was about to tell her about his talk with Reynaldo at Smoke Alley when a soft horn toot interrupted.

"Salutations! How go the preparations?" came a polished voice. Gordon Hollenbeck flashed them a smile as he and Gerald pulled up in their tiny red Daihatsu.

"Just about done here," Lucky said. "Need to board up one window in the back by the fill station, but then I'll need to head back home and get things sorted there."

"We're going to gas up before the station runs dry," Gerald said. "Happy to give your young charges a lift back to Windwardside."

Boone looked to Lucky, who nodded. "Sure. We'll be done by the time you get back." As the two men drove ahead, passing to the left of the Customs and Immigration building, Lucky gathered his tools. "The only gas station on the island is up that road at Big Rock Engineering. I gassed up this morning. Once they run out, it might be a while before we get another shipment in, depending on where the hurricane hits."

"What do Sabans do if they run out of gas?" Emily asked.

"I haven't been here long enough to see that happen, but ... they walk. Just like they did before The Road. The island is full of trails between the villages."

————◆ • ◆————

The Servant selected two of the better trail maps that he'd stolen the week before, adding them to the backpack, along with the forged documents and a few bottles of water he decided he could spare. He'd delivered plenty of water for Gunter the last time and the supermarkets were completely out now. A small offering of additional water might go a long way toward facilitating a smooth handover of the money he was due. And, in case things *didn't* go so smoothly, he slid the machete in as well. The Servant crouched by his prisoner, gently lifting her chin to look into her eyes. He had just used the last of his supply of sedatives, but after this delivery he wouldn't need them anymore. He would remain with her until The Ascent. They would need to leave early, to be in place before the winds made the climb impossible. Fortunately, Mount Scenery had a concrete building at the base of a communications tower near the summit, the ideal shelter for him once he had performed the ritual. He withdrew his hand from the girl's face, letting her head loll forward. "Now, don't go anywhere."

Ascending the stairs, the Servant pulled the paint tarp across the door to the cellar and headed for his vehicle.

◆　◆

"I told our landlady we'd help get Hummingbird Haven ready for Irma today," Emily said. "S'okay if you handsome gentlemen take us through town to the English Quarter?"

"Sure, not a problem," Gerald said, tapping the horn for a toot as he reached a switchback above The Bottom.

"Do you two need help boarding up?" Boone asked.

"Oh, thank you, dear boy, but ours is one of the sturdiest homes on the island. The hurricane shutters are quite easy to secure, and we're snug up against a slope. Actually, Gerald and I were talking; Amber's Hummingbird Haven cottage is quite lovely but it's fairly exposed. We'd be more than happy to take you two in for the duration of the blow."

"That's very generous. Honestly, I've never had to weather a storm like this, Bonaire being out of the Hurricane Belt."

"Well, to be equally honest, we haven't had to deal with many," Gerald said. "We missed the bigger ones: Georges back in '98 and José and Lenny in '99—they were before we moved to Saba. Earl back in 2010 was pretty much a tropical storm down here." He chuckled. "Ironically, biggest hurricane I've ever been in was Sandy when I was visiting my mother in New York."

"Well, if it's not too much trouble…" Emily began.

"No trouble at all, my dear," Gordon assured. "I invite some of my Broadway buddies down from time to time, so we have two guest rooms you can choose from. Plus, you can help us keep our dear little pup Juniper from getting too scared. I'm afraid her Thundershirt might not be enough for a Cat 4!"

"Awww … we'd love to protect your pooch. What breed is she?"

"Yorkipoo. Although she thinks she's part wolf, where socks are involved. Don't leave yours unattended!"

"What are these socks you speak of?" From the back seat, Emily raised a shapely leg and waggled her toes in her sandals.

Dropping Boone and Emily at the rental cottage, Gordon and Gerald suggested they all meet at the Bizzy B Bakery in the morning. Amber Linzey was around the side of the cottage by the overlook, bringing in a pair of hummingbird feeders. Spotting the young couple, she raised one aloft by way of greeting.

"Have you been here long?" Emily asked.

"No, no, just got here," Amber said. "I went to the supermarket as soon as they opened, and I just finished securing my cottage in Hell's Gate."

"By the way, Gordon Hollenbeck and Gerald..." Boone began, before trailing off. "Y'know, we've never learned his last name."

"Marland," Amber provided.

"Thanks. They offered to let us stay over during the storm."

"Oh, that's wonderful! I was going to suggest you stay at *my* place in Hell's Gate but their cottage is quite solid and tucked into the hillside, and mine's very small." She gestured at the rental cottage. "Hummingbird has a beautiful view, but she's so exposed out here."

A series of bleats, some quite human-sounding, came from a thick stand of yellow-orange flowers.

"Get out of my black-eyed Susans, you little goat bastards!" Amber took a few steps toward the flowers and a couple of tiny goats bounded away. "You too, Crybaby. I see you in there." Amber took another step and the tiniest goat of the bunch dashed after its pals.

"Aww, they're adorable!"

"Sure they are ... until they eat your garden down to the roots. Saba has more goats than people. Good thing they're delicious."

"Nooooo..." Emily whined.

"Oh, come on Em. You had goat curry in Bonaire," Boone reminded her.

"Yeah but ... that was just some tasty brown stuff in a bowl, it wasn't bouncing around looking all cute. Hey, Amber, you have so many goats, you should make Saba the Goat Yoga travel destination of the world!"

"Goat Yoga?" Amber asked with a raised eyebrow. "What's that?"

"It's just yoga," Boone said. "But with goats."

"You oversimplify everything!" Emily scolded. "See, the goats like to be up high, so when you do some yoga poses, they jump up on your back and just stand there with their wittle hooves. Usually you end up laughing. A *lot*. And that's as good for you as the yoga."

"People pay money to let goats stand on them?" Amber asked, unconvinced. "What if they take a shit?"

Boone burst into laughter. "That ever happen, Em?"

Emily bit her lip. "Um … yes…? But it just made me laugh harder, so…"

"Hey, can you eat these?" Boone asked, walking over to a bush than ran along a white picket fence. The green, orange, and red fruits that hung from it were berry-sized and had an interesting shape, with little flanges or ribs down the side like miniature pumpkins.

"You can. Suriname cherries are a bit of an acquired taste, but they make a good jam. I recommend you stick to the red ones, unless you like sour and bitter. They have a big seed in them, so fair warning."

Boone plucked two red ones, popping one in his mouth as he tossed another to Emily, who caught it and took a bite.

"Oh, my!" Emily said, puckering a bit. "Don't know that I'd call them *cherries*. They have a tart little kick after the sweet."

"Actually, they're related to guava, cloves, and allspice."

"I think I'll stick to soursop and mangos," Emily concluded.

Boone looked around the grounds of the cottage. "Let us know what we can do," he offered.

"First, help me bring in the patio furniture, hummingbird feeders, tools, anything you see that might blow away."

"Have you been through a storm on Saba?" Emily asked.

"A couple, but it's been a while since we had a big one. I was here for Wrong Way Lenny. Most hurricanes travel westward, but that one formed over by Jamaica and came east toward the Leewards. Fortunately, the damage wasn't that bad. Georges, on the other hand ... have you seen those ruined buildings near Juliana's Hotel?"

"Yeah, Gordon gave us a tour and we walked by those," Boone said.

"Hurricane Georges did that. Used to be a hotel, the Captain's Quarters. Scout's Place, where we met, was damaged too. Hospital and airport lost their roofs. The thing about Saba ... since we're basically on a mountain, we're protected from the main threat from hurricanes: the storm surge. Low-lying islands like Saint Martin, they can suffer a lot of flooding. But the trade-off is, we're high up, and the higher you are, the stronger the winds."

"I was wondering about that," Boone said as he gathered up a pair of deck chairs.

"Not only that, but the way the interior is shaped, sometimes the winds can be funneled, almost like a tornado."

"How did your cottages hold up?" Emily asked.

"Well, I didn't own Hummingbird Haven then, but I heard she lost her roof. My place in Hell's Gate managed to keep its roof, but barely. I remember being huddled on the bathroom floor holding the door closed while the wind pulled at it." She looked at them abruptly. "But there were no deaths, scary as it was. We're an island full of people descended from shipbuilders, so our buildings are incredibly sturdy. Most cottages, every wall joint has extra support." She retrieved the last of the hummingbird feeders. "But let's just hope Irma weakens or stays north of us. That being said, will you help me secure the shutters?"

An hour later, Boone and Emily walked back along The Road toward Windwardside. "I forgot to ask … how'd the training with Sophie go? I saw her down at the airport and she said you were a quick study."

"What, you needed *her* to tell you that?" Emily gasped, playfully shouldering Boone. "She's a great teacher! I learned a boatload of Krav Maga moves and she gave me some exercises to do. Of course, it's not as flashy as your capybara."

"That's a South American rodent."

"Is it?" Emily grinned impishly at him from beneath her sunglasses. "Anyhoo, I'm going to make this a regular Sunday practice, schedule permitting."

They reached the main intersection in Windwardside and Emily came to a sudden halt by the white picket fence in front of Saba Snack. She stared at the dining patio, then looked across at the supermarket.

"Em, what's up?" Boone asked.

"Nothing," she said, somewhat absently. "I just remembered; we had a spot of bother with a looky-loo while we were eating. Dodgy bloke, gave off a real creepy vibe."

Boone felt a prickle at his scalp as he turned to Emily. "What did he look like?"

"Umm … white guy. Stonking big. Almost as tall as you, but broader. I think he was muscly, but it was hard to tell with the baggy work clothes he was wearing."

"Like coveralls?" Boone asked with increasing urgency. "Gray?"

Emily removed her sunglasses. "Yeah…" she said quietly.

"What color hair?"

"Blond."

Suddenly, everything clicked into place and Boone grabbed her hand. "Come on. Let's see if Sid's here."

"Wait, why? Who *was* that guy?"

They stepped into the police annex. Sid was at his desk with a cell phone in his hand. He held up a finger when Boone and Emily entered. "Yes, okay, thank you." He hung up. "Irma has strengthened a bit." He saw the urgency on Boone's face. "What's the matter?"

"Do you remember that break-in at the trail shop?"

"*Alleged* break-in," Sid corrected.

Boone waved that away. "Do you remember the man I told you about? The one who was crossing the street from the trail shop?"

"Yeah, the guy dressed like a workman?" Sid recalled.

"Or a painter," Emily suggested. Boone looked at her and she shrugged. "He had yellow paint on him, I think."

Something about that comment tickled a memory in Boone's mind but he filed it away as he told Sid his theory. "This man I saw ... the one that Gordon—who knows everyone—didn't recognize ... I felt there was something *off* about him. I let it go, figuring I was picking up on something that wasn't really there. But over on Statia, Reynaldo said a white male, tall and blond, had tried to book passage with him to Saba. He refused him, but then watched the man go across to two smugglers on the *Wavy Davey*." Boone slipped a finger under the cord on his neck. "And Rey said the man had one of *these*."

"Holy shit," Sid muttered, sitting up straight in his chair.

"So this blond stranger comes over here ... from Statia, where they just had a girl go missing ... and a few weeks later *you* have a young couple go missing. And what do we find at the last place we think they were?"

185

"A Statian Blue Bead," Sid whispered. Then he shook his head. "But we don't know for sure our missing couple was at the customs house."

"We know *someone* was. With two flashlights. And likely enjoying the same kind of beers that couple was seen buying that evening."

"And you think this man had something to do with their disappearance?"

"Yes. I do. *And* the girl on Statia. And … there was a girl on Saint Kitts, too, the month before *that*."

Sid chewed his lip. "Look, I admit, this *feels* right … but we haven't seen any sign of our missing couple. And as for the mystery man…"

"Emily saw him yesterday," Boone said.

"Wait, what? When?"

Emily was still processing everything Boone had just said, feeling a bit lost in the flood of information. She blinked. "Oh … right … sorry … yeah, early afternoon. Sophie, Anika, and I caught him staring at us. He went across to the supermarket."

"The time I saw him he got into a black SUV," Boone recalled, "parked at the bottom of the Mount Scenery stairs. If we can find that vehicle…"

Sid sighed. "We've got a severe hurricane on the way and we don't have the resources to do a major search. It could be anywhere."

"Yellow paint…" Boone said.

"What?"

"Emily said…" He looked up, excited. "Sid, that picture of you and Sophie at the sulphur mine, can you pull it up?"

"Um … sure?" Sid scrolled through his photos and found it, handing the phone to Boone.

Zooming in, Boone found what he was looking for. "Emily, did the paint look like this?" He held up the phone.

"Yes! I remember now, it wasn't exactly like paint. That's it!"

Sid took the phone and examined the photo. "The walls of the tunnels are coated in sulphur deposits, and it's pretty cramped in there. Not hard to get some on your clothes."

"One of the maps that went missing from the trail shop was from the mine, right? And you said a lot of the tunnels were closed off," Boone recalled. "I think I know where this guy is hiding."

20

It was breezier today, the Servant noted. Not surprising, with what lay over the eastern horizon. He hefted his backpack and started down the trail toward the mine. He had left his vehicle at the dead end of Sulphur Mine Road in Upper Hell's Gate and was only a few hundred yards along the trail when he heard the sound of a car on the road above. Maybe two. Then the unmistakable slams of multiple car doors, followed by voices. Scrambling off the trail and up the slope to his left, the Servant hunkered down in dense foliage surrounding the base of a thick gumbo-limbo. After a few minutes, the voices grew closer. Two policemen wearing bullet-proof vests, one of them with a shotgun, came down the trail, along with a Dutch marine carrying an assault rifle. Accompanying them was a civilian, a tall, lanky man who looked familiar. *Last week at the trail shop. He was the one staring at me.* Silently, the Servant cursed his ill luck. If that man remembered the SUV he'd been driving, he might have recognized it parked above.

The group passed by and the Servant remained still and silent. The group was speaking in low voices and he couldn't make out anything they said, but it was clear they were heading down the slopes to the abandoned sulphur mine. *So much for Gunter,* he thought. *So much for my payment. No matter. Whatever I need will be provided.* Once the group had vanished from sight below him, the Servant carefully made his way to the trail and headed back to his vehicle, stopping just short of the stairs that ascended to the road. More voices. One voice was feminine, youthful, with some form of British accent. *I know that voice.* He left the trail again, angling toward a steep section of slope to get a vantage point of the dead end. Again, he heard the girl's voice. He found a spot where a number of roots provided excellent handholds. Before beginning the short climb, he adjusted the contents of his backpack, ensuring the duct-taped hilt was easily accessible.

———————◆ ◆ ◆———————

"Mind you, I think it's bollocks to get left behind ... I mean, why does Boone get to go? On the other hand, I've never been a fan of caves. Well, except underwater caves. Love those. Why is that, do you think, that I'm creeped out by land caves, but if I'm in a far-more-dangerous underwater one, that's actually fun for me? Swim-throughs are the best. You ever go diving? You should, you know, while you're here." Emily took a breath. "I'm talking a lot, aren't I?"

The Royal Dutch Marine smiled. "Maybe a little," he said. He was younger than Emily and his command of English was borderline at best.

"I guess I'm just nervous. If that bad guy really is in there..."

"Ach, do not worry. If he is, Johann vill take care of him. He is best shot in our unit."

Emily noted the assault rifle this young soldier carried. "Why aren't *you* with them? I mean ... two giant scary guns are better than one, right?"

The young man laughed. "Your friend, he say to stay vith you. In case they miss 'bad guy', and he come back for his car." He nodded toward the black SUV parked ahead of the two Saba police cars. "If he does, I stop him."

◆ • ◆

Peering over the crest, the Servant glowered at the scene before him. He recalled a line from a movie, about the folly of bringing a knife to a gunfight. Pitting his machete against that assault rifle would be suicide. Besides, his vehicle was likely what had led them here in the first place, and there was nothing of value in it. He would return to his hideaway on foot. His eyes lingered on the beautiful, young blonde. Under five feet, skin tanned and glowing with vitality, her blond hair dangling in a shining ponytail. *So much like Lucy. She is perfect.* But before the voices could bubble up and berate him, he lowered his eyes from the road and started back down toward the trail. Below, there was a sign at an intersection and he paused there to consult one of the stolen maps. To the right, the trail to The Sulphur Mine. To the left, the All Too Far Trail. He went left. From there, the North Coast Trail would take him to the western side of Saba, and the Middle Island Trail would bring him the rest of the way to the unfinished cottage and his prisoner. The girl he had selected was not quite his type, but she was the Chosen for this island, and she would suffice. Tomorrow evening, he would Ascend.

The entrance to the mine was a dark hole in the hillside, and Boone felt a chill as he looked at it, although that could just be the brisk breeze that was coming in from the east. He crouched, eyeing the loose scree around the opening—it wasn't the kind of surface to hold tracks. Still, he didn't need to see any signs to know they were in the right place. On the way down the trail, Boone had convinced Captain Every that the SUV parked near the head of the trail was definitely the one he'd seen the blond man in the coveralls drive away in.

"Sid, with your busted rib, I'd feel better if you weren't crawling around in there," Sid's father said. "Stay here with the shotgun and be our lookout. The way those tunnels go, he might come around behind us and make a break for it. And Boone, you stay with him."

"You may need me," Boone replied.

"No. You're a civilian."

"All due respect, sir, I can handle myself. And going into a bunch of dark tunnels with just two men doesn't seem like a good idea."

Captain Every blew a blast of air through his mustache. He had debated waiting for more backup, but the small police force was already strained, preparing for the storm. They were fortunate to have borrowed a couple of the Royal Marines as it was. "Fine. You bring up the rear, though. And Sid, give him your vest."

Boone held up a hand. "Actually, sir, I think Johann should have that, if you're planning on putting him in the lead."

Sid handed the Dutch marine his bulletproof vest while Captain Every described the layout of the tunnels nearest the entrance. "We'll have to crabwalk right at the beginning. Most of the mine is blocked off by a gate on the left side of the main tunnel, but there are plenty of places to hide in the accessible areas. Right inside the entrance, it will split. To the right is a cramped side passage. Sid, if he comes up that way, you'll be able to see him, so if that happens, fire a warning shot and order him to lie down in the entrance. If we're deep inside, the radios might not work, so that shot will let us know. Now, I want to keep together, no one solo, so we'll take the main entrance on the left and make a circuit." The captain placed a hand on the young marine's shoulder. "Johann, it's single file in there most of the time, so I'll need you up front with your weapon."

"Not a problem," the young marine said, pocketing his beret and strapping on the headlamp Captain Every had provided him.

"Boone … here." Sid offered his headlamp and Boone took it.

Captain Every patted a small cylinder on his duty belt that Boone had assumed was tear gas. "If we corner him, and he's armed, I've got this flash bang. In a cramped, pitch-black tunnel it will *not* be pleasant so if I shout *flash*, shut your eyes and cover your ears *immediately*. One more thing, it's hot in there. *Very* hot. So take it slow," Captain Every drew his pistol and hefted a MagLite. "All right, let's go."

For the first minute or two Boone almost had to crawl, and even after the passageway opened up, his height forced him to walk hunched over. He gave a mental chuckle. *Emily would have been better suited for this.*

"Okay, here's the sealed portion of the mines," Captain Every said, shining his flashlight on a padlocked yellow gate. Behind it lay a small, dusty chamber. With the thin metal bars of the grating across the opening, it almost looked like a dungeon cell. At the back wall, another tunnel led into darkness. The captain played his light back there, but the beam barely penetrated the gloom. "When a tourist got lost up there and died, they closed this off. If someone wanted to hide back there they'd need to get through this," Captain Every said, shining the light on a padlock covered in dust and grime. Gripping the padlock, he gave it a tug to test it. "Locked."

"Who has keys?" Boone asked.

"I have one and the Saba Conservation Foundation has another, but no one else. Let's keep moving."

Johann and Captain Every led the way and Boone followed, the air becoming noticeably hotter. Boone suddenly stopped in his tracks as the lights of the others receded into the blackness ahead. *Something ... changed.* He turned and slowly made his way back to the gate. Crouching down, he looked at the padlock. *Sid's father grabbed it ... and after ... something changed.* He peered more closely. *There.* Two little spots of silver.

"Boone?" Captain Every's harsh whisper echoed from the tunnel ahead.

Boone didn't answer, focused on the lock. Lifting it in his hand, he spat on its flank and rubbed the dirty surface with a thumb. The dirt came right off, revealing the shiny silver of a brand-new lock.

"Boone!"

Boone looked toward the captain's voice, reaching up to his headlamp. Finding the switch, he flicked it off and on. If the man they sought was behind this gate, Boone thought it best not to shout into an echo chamber about what he had discovered. When Boone's face was illuminated by the returning men, he raised a finger to his lips, then defaulted by instinct to diver hand signals, pointing two fingers to his eyes, then pointing at the lock. *Look there.*

Captain Every crouched and looked at the shiny lock as Boone rubbed more of the grime away. "That's not the regular lock," the captain said in a low voice. "And if Croc Johnson had changed it, he would have let us know and given us a new key."

"Someone covered it in dirt," Boone said quietly.

"Do we shoot it off?" Johann asked.

"Too much chance of a ricochet," Captain Every said. "I'll have Sid radio for some bolt cutters."

"Not just yet," Boone said, examining the rest of the gate. There were patches of rust in many places and the lock plate itself looked somewhat the worse for wear. "Johann, this is going to sound like an odd question. What size boot do you wear?"

"Forty-four."

"European size, right? Umm … any idea…?"

"Oh, in U.S. size? About an eleven, I think. Why do you want to know?"

Boone looked with longing at Johann's combat boots, knowing they would never fit his size thirteen feet. "Never mind. Was hoping for a little extra padding. I'll just have to do this a bit differently. Stand back. And Captain, can you put your light on the padlock?"

Crouching in the tunnel, Boone placed himself almost at the far wall across from the gate. Planting his hands on the ground, he stretched his long legs out, eyes on the lock plate. The *martelo de negativa* was considered one of the strongest kicks in all martial arts with regard to the amount of force striking the target. Executed from the ground with most of the body's mass devoted to the kick, some practitioners were able to deliver nearly a ton of force. The problem here was that he was wearing sport sandals and it was usually the instep that struck the target. Boone wasn't about to smash the top of his sandaled foot into metal, but the soles were quite sturdy, so he would need to pivot the ankle and focus the kick through the heel. *No problem*, he thought, though the strength of his conviction left a bit to be desired.

Taking a moment to focus his mind, Boone took six deep breaths, ignoring the hint of sulphur in the air. Then he coiled his muscles and unleashed his body, swinging his legs up, the upper leg continuing through the air with a whoosh. The heel of his foot smashed into the plate to the left of the lock, the impact bending it and popping the other end free of the gate.

"*Ongelofelijk...*" Johann exclaimed quietly, stepping forward to inspect the damage.

Captain Every reached out and gave the gate a shove. It squeaked in metallic protest but swung inward. "Okay, if he's back there he may have heard that, so let's—"

Suddenly, a blinding flash and earsplitting roar erupted from the tunnel on the far side of the gated chamber—the muzzle flash and reports from a semi-automatic rifle. Johann yelped in surprise, falling to the right of the opening. Boone grabbed Captain Every and hurled himself to the left side of the gate. Sparkling puffs of yellow sulphur and purple gypsum erupted from the tunnel wall opposite the gate as rounds tore into it.

"Cack ... that's going to leave a mark," the captain hissed through gritted teeth.

"Where are you hit?" Boone asked urgently.

"Arm," Captain Every grunted, clearly in pain. "Lost my pistol..."

"Johann? Are you hit?"

A groan was the prone Dutchman's only response. Boone's headlamp could just make out the soles of the man's boots further up the tunnel. The marine's assault rifle was not in sight, but Captain Every's service weapon lay squarely in front of the gate. Boone extended a long arm across the floor but that invited another burst of fire, and he swiftly pulled his hand back. *Well, that's not going to work.* Boone focused his headlamp on the captain's wound—there was a growing bloom of bright blood on the upper arm. From the distant entrance of the mine, they could hear Sid calling out.

"Can you get back to Sid?" Boone asked.

"Yes, I think so. But we can't leave Johann."

"We won't. Here, trade you." Boone pulled the headlamp off and pushed it into the captain's hands, scooping the policeman's MagLite from the floor of the tunnel. "I'll need this, too," he said, plucking the flashbang from Captain Every's duty belt as the man rose unsteadily to his feet.

"Pull the pin and toss it, just like a grenade," the captain said quietly, his face clammy with sweat. "You'll have one and a half seconds before it goes off." He staggered away toward the entrance.

Boone could hear movement in the tunnel beyond the chamber. *He's moving forward. Maybe I can throw him off.* "Whoever you are," he called out, "we just want the boy and girl back. You let them go, we let *you* go!"

The sounds of movement stopped. "Girl und boy? Vat ze hell are you talking about?"

Wait a minute, the shooter sounds … German? Then that means … he's the other smuggler. "Listen, we're not here for you. We're looking for the man you brought over from Statia."

"He's not here!"

"That man is probably a murderer. Don't protect him. His car is at the head of the trail."

"*Vas? Gott verdammt, meine* papers!"

Boone heard the man's footsteps again and he knew the smuggler was going to make a break for it, likely shooting Boone and finishing off Johann in the process. *No more time.* In an instant, he envisioned a sequence of actions and set them in motion. He tossed the MagLite toward Captain Every's pistol, the flash-light's beam facing the gate. He shut his eyes just before the expected burst of automatic weapon's fire occurred. Boone was already pulling the pin on the stun grenade before the burst finished, opening his eyes for a brief moment as he tossed the device between the nearest bars of the gate, aiming for the mouth of the exit tunnel at the back of the blocked-off chamber. He turned away, clamping his eyes shut as hard as he could while pressing his palms over his ears with all of his strength.

Despite these precautions, the explosion was deafening in the close confines of the mine, and the white flash of light was visible through his eyelids. Even with his ears ringing, he had no trouble hearing a high, keening sound—the smuggler shrieking in agony. Opening his eyes, Boone sprang to the gate and kicked it sharply, sending it swinging back into the chamber with a crash. The MagLite was pointed into an empty corner of the room but in the edge of its beam, Boone spotted movement. The smuggler was clearly stunned and clawing at something on his face. *Night-vision goggles! The explosion from the flashbang must have fried his retinas.* On the floor lay an assault rifle, identical to the one they had found on the *Wavy Davey* when they'd gone after the submarine.

"*Meine augen!*" the German shrieked, managing to tear the goggles from his head. Boone reached him in two long strides, scooping up the rifle and slamming the butt against the man's temple. The smuggler crumpled to the floor. *Got to see to Johann before I can deal with this asshole,* he thought. *Too bad I didn't think to grab some cuffs off the captain.* He dashed back to the gate but stopped when he heard the unmistakable sound of a pump-action shotgun being racked. After a flash of fear that the mysterious blond man was in here after all, Boone suddenly remembered what Sid had been carrying. Then, the young Saban cop's voice confirmed it.

"Whoever you are, toss your weapon out and step into the tunnel!"

"Sid, it's Boone!"

A headlamp flicked on and started toward the gate. "Boone! Where's the shooter?"

"He's down. Behind the gate at the back of the room. Cuff him in case he comes to, but I'm guessing that flash bang scrambled his marbles pretty damn good. Me bashing him in the head probably didn't do him any favors, either. I need to check on Johann!"

"Ja, please do…" came a choked voice from down the tunnel. "If it's not too much trouble."

"Johann, thank God," Boone said, crawling to the fallen marine. "You didn't answer before. I thought maybe—"

"I hit my head on the damn wall falling back from the shooting. Embarrassing, really."

"It's pretty cramped in here—easy to see how it could happen. You're not hit?"

"No, don't think so." He retrieved his weapon and got to his feet. "I am okay to walk."

"Sid, how's your dad?" Boone called out.

"He'll be fine. It was a through-and-through and he's got direct pressure on it. Paramedics are on their way."

"Good. Okay, then, let's grab that bastard and get the hell out of here."

———◆·◆———

"It's not him," Emily said, as they stood around the police cars at the dead end above the sulphur mine. The paramedics had taken

Sid's father away and the smuggler sat in the low grass on the side of the road, cuffed and sullen.

"I know it's not," Boone said, looking at the man. "But he's one of the smugglers who brought him over, so maybe he knows where he is."

"Vhat?" the smuggler shouted. His vision had more or less returned, but his hearing was another matter.

"Do you know where the kidnapper is?" Boone said slowly and loudly. "The one you brought over from Statia."

"*Nein*," the German said. "And I don't know vere your missing people are. He never told me about any kidnapping. I paid him to bring me food und vater."

"What was his name?" Boone asked.

"No idea. He never said and I never asked. I never let him past the gate. He was *gruselig* … How would you say? Creepy. I did not trust him."

Johann had been examining the smuggler's night-vision goggles. "Boone, you are lucky these are a civilian model. Military-grade ones might have blocked the glare and protected him. He could have shot you before you reached him."

"Gunter Schleich," Sid shouted, reading a card from the man's wallet. "Where is your stash?"

"I don't know vat you are talking about."

"Really?" Boone said, amused. "Because your buddy Santiago said you took the other bag."

"*Das Schwein!*" Gunter cursed.

"Thought so."

"We'll find it," Sid said. "Saba Conservation has people who know those tunnels as well as anyone. But that still doesn't help us with the man they brought over." He turned to the policeman who had joined them, a black Saban with a broad chest and well-formed arms. The man was going through the SUV's glove compartment. "George, you find anything?"

"Not much. No papers in da glove box. Dere some tarps aback and a painter's bucket with some brushes and rollers." He got out and slammed the passenger door, the sound seeming to knock a memory loose. "O-me-gracious, you know what? You know dat day you had us canvassing for witnesses up Ladder Road? I just figured out where I see dis auto."

"Where?" Sid asked urgently.

The Servant was drenched in sweat by the time he climbed off the Middle Island Trail to the end of Ladder Road. He was only fifty yards from the trailhead when he stopped in his tracks. Flashing lights ahead. Voices raised. *No! No, no, no, no!* He quickly slipped into the thick greenery on the slope to his left and made his way closer.

"It was parked right here, with tools and a stepladder," George said after Sid pulled up behind the other policeman's squad car and exited with Boone and Emily. The young Dutch marine who had stayed behind with Emily back at the sulphur mine was standing guard beside the constable, weapon poised in a ready position, finger resting against the lower receiver above the trigger. Boone had no doubt the man could bring it to bear in an instant.

They had all driven across the length of the island and were now standing in the driveway of an unfinished cottage.

Boone looked around. The overall feel was of a place that was having some maintenance done on it, but his gut told him otherwise. He stepped up to an unfinished wall and looked inside. There was nothing in view but some painter's tarps and piles of lumber.

The constable joined him. "It looked like dis when I was here before, canvassing da neighborhood. I called out but no one answered."

"Something…" Boone said, trailing off. *There's a lot of dust on the tarps in here. Except for …* Not bothering with the doorway, he vaulted across a section of skeletal wall and into the interior, going straight to a clear plastic tarp that was hung along an interior wall. He pulled it aside. A door.

The Servant reached a thick stand of elephant ears, the massive leaves of the plant providing excellent cover. He crouched, eyes on the cottage. Two police cars. A soldier stood out front, cradling an assault rifle across his chest. It looked like the same one who had been beside the Servant's vehicle above the sulphur mine. No one else was in sight but there were two police cars beside the driveway.

"She's here!" a voice cried out. The soldier turned, nodding to someone inside the cottage.

No! The Servant's vision went white with rage. *It's too close! There's no time!* Without realizing he'd done it, his hand had found the taped hilt of the machete and drawn it from his backpack. *If I can get that soldier's weapon...*

A young policeman appeared inside the cottage beside an open section of wall, speaking to someone behind him. "No sign of the boy. Or the kidnapper."

If I'm going to do this, it has to be now! The Servant rose from his crouch ... and froze.

"Come on, easy does it. You're safe now." The feminine voice was soft and soothing. And British. Exiting the cottage, the beautiful little blonde emerged, her arms around a softly weeping figure.

You. You ... bitch! The Servant watched helplessly as the two young women were joined by two policemen and the tall, lanky man from before. *All of you!* In less than twenty-four hours, he would have been Ascending, all the signs pointing to a successful ritual, but now these people had ruined everything. He focused his frustration on the petite blonde, the one that looked so much like Lucy. And from inside his mind, a voice: *All is not lost. The answer is right in front of you.*

The Servant uncoiled his muscles, sinking back into the greenery. *Yes ... it would be fitting.* And perhaps this was the plan all along. She *was* the perfect sacrifice, in his eyes. Perhaps those he served had been testing him, and now they had *allowed* his original Chosen to be rescued—and not rescued by just anyone. No, this all seemed ... *purposeful.*

He thought back to the snatches of conversation he had overheard from the girl and her two friends when they were having lunch. *The English Quarter.* She was staying in that neighborhood on the other side of Windwardside. But where exactly was the cottage? *It had a name ... what was it?*

Suddenly, a flash of movement caught his eye, and the Servant turned toward a yellow stand of black-eyed Susans. Above, clusters of red hibiscus flowers dangled down. The flash of movement happened again, this time coming to a relative stop, as an object came to a hover beside the flowers. A hummingbird. The Servant smiled. Once again, those he served had provided. *Thank you. I remember now.*

21

"Dear me, that sounds positively awful," Gordon Hollenbeck said, after Boone briefly described the battle in the sulphur mine. "You couldn't *pay* me to go into those caves, with my claustrophobia."

"It's true. He doesn't even like to go into the dryer for the last sock," Gerald teased.

"It was only that one time!"

Gerald winked at him before turning to Boone. "How's your hearing?"

"Pretty much back to normal. Can't say the same for the smuggler."

"And they didn't find his friend?"

"He swears he didn't know where the man was on the island. I got the impression he didn't much care for him."

"I only saw him for about ten seconds and I didn't care for him," Emily muttered.

The four were sitting in the little plaza by the Bizzy B, enjoying what might be the last fresh bread for a while. Irma was scheduled to arrive early the following morning. Already, the winds had picked up in Windwardside, though at the moment it was hard to believe there was a major Category 5 hurricane over the horizon. The bakery's ovens had been working overtime, and Gerald and Gordon—or *Double G,* as Emily had taken to calling them—had procured an entire bag of croissants for the days ahead. It was almost noon. After the events of the previous day, Boone had called them to ask if they could nudge their early rendezvous to a bit later in the morning.

"How is the girl doing?" Gerald inquired.

"Considering what she went through, she's doing well," Emily said. "I stayed with her and her parents at the hospital for a while last night."

"And the young man? Any clues as to his whereabouts?" Gordon asked.

"No," she said, her voice sobering further. "But it doesn't look good. She thinks the man killed him."

"Sid says, once the storm has passed, the police will mount a wider search," Boone said. "For the kidnapper, too."

"Well, at least you got the villain's vehicle!" Gordon said.

"Yeah, spot of luck there," Emily said.

"It'll be a lot harder for him to get around," Gerald remarked. "Not likely he'll risk hitchhiking, with the police searching for him."

"Unless he's using the trails…" Boone mused.

"Well, he'd better enjoy them while he can. Once Irma hits, those trails will become mud and fallen limbs."

"What's in the bottle?" Emily asked, pointing at an unlabeled liter bottle filled with brown liquid beside the bag of croissants. "Looks like flat soda."

"Well, since there's no telling how long we'll be holed up at Chez Hollenbeck," Gordon said, "we headed over to Lucy Hassell's to grab some of her homemade specialty. This is Saba Spice, one of the island's traditional products, the other being Saba Lace. Everyone's Spice is a little different, but it's basically a high-proof rum infused with cinnamon, fennel, cloves, and brown sugar."

"I like it on vanilla ice cream," Gerald said. "In fact, just in case we lose power, we probably should have that tonight."

"Sounds scrummy!" Emily said. "So, what time do you want us there?"

"Any time is fine. Gordon and I made up both guest rooms, in case we find any additional wayward strays. Curfew is ten p.m., I heard."

"Well, I suppose we can run back to the Hummingbird Haven now and fetch our things," Boone said, rising from the table. "See you in a few?"

"The welcome mat will be unfurled," Gordon intoned.

By late afternoon, Boone and Emily arrived at the home of the Double Gs. Sure enough, there was a welcome mat with the words *Ring the bell, and I shall sing you the song of my people. Sincerely, The Dog.* There wasn't a doorbell, but a light rap on the doorframe brought a high-pitched burst of barking and a little tuft-eared pooch, smaller than most cats, came into view. A furiously wagging nub of a tail was at odds with the bark, but she dashed out of sight when Gerald let the couple in.

"That was Juniper, a.k.a. Junie, a.k.a. Nipper. She can be a bit people-shy but she'll warm up to you in no time. Gordon's in the cellar, conquering his fears with the washer and dryer. Come along. I'll give you the nickel tour and you can pick a guest room."

After a quick once-through, Boone brought the bags into the guest room Emily had selected.

"Why'd you choose this one?" Boone asked.

"Bigger bed."

Boone arched an eyebrow.

"Not for bonking! The other room, your feet would've dangled off the end."

"Oh," Boone said, coloring his voice with a touch of disappointment.

Emily traced a finger along his arm. "That being said ... a little 'how's your father' in a hurricane might take our minds off impending doom."

A knock came at the door. "I have something for you." Gordon held out a pair of lanyards.

Emily took them. "Whistles?"

"Just a precaution. As I said, our cottage is very sturdy, like most of the construction on Saba. All the same, I thought it might be wise for everyone to have one of these, just in case everything goes pear-shaped."

Emily held one up. "Lime green! How did you know?"

"I'm a former Broadway dresser, my dear. I have an eye for clothes, and you have a particular palette preference."

"What gave me away, my stylish trainers?" Emily asked, raising a sockless foot and waggling her lime green tennis shoes. She slid the lanyard over her head and tucked the whistle into her tank top. "Here Boone, you get pink."

Boone grinned, dropping the lanyard around his neck. "Like a Bonaire flamingo. Hey, I think I'll head over to the police annex, see if Sid found out anything else. Wanna come?"

Emily's reply was arrested by a jingling sound as Juniper the Yorkipoo made her entrance, charging after a miniature tennis ball and skidding to a halt as the toy rolled against Emily's foot. "I dunno, Boone ... I may need to stay here and commune with this little lady. Hey, wittle snookums, you want your ball?"

The pup crouched at attention, tail wagging, as Emily rolled the ball across the floor. Juniper dashed after it, claws scrabbling on the wooden floors.

"Give Sid my best," Emily said with a grin, scampering after the little dog.

———— ✦ • ✦ ————

"What's the latest on Irma?" Boone asked as he entered the little annex.

Sid looked up from his computer, his face uncharacteristically grim. "It's not looking good. Let me refresh." He clicked the touchpad and waited, shaking his head at the information that appeared. "Holy ... 178 miles per hour. She's been a strong Category 5 since this morning, but that's just..." He opened another window on the screen and looked at a chart. "The Saffir-Simpson Scale has a Cat 5 starting at 157, and this is over 20 miles per hour above that! If there were such a thing as a Category 6, Irma would be in the running."

Boone grabbed a chair from opposite Sid's desk and dragged it around to look at the laptop. "Is this the strongest you've experienced?"

Sid barked a rueful laugh. "Boone, this is probably the strongest *anyone* in the Leewards has experienced." He pointed at the map. "And I wouldn't want to be *here*."

Boone leaned in to look. "Barbuda."

"Current track forecasts a direct hit there just after midnight and Barbuda is mostly at sea level. The saving grace on Saba is our geography. Storm surge is the number one killer in a hurricane and there's no chance of that here. Well, except in Fort Bay ... but there are no residences there and it will be entirely evacuated."

"What time do they expect Irma will reach Saba?"

"There's still room for error, but probably around seven or eight in the morning. Track is taking the eye a bit north of us, but the storm is well over 300 miles wide, so we'll almost certainly be in heavy wind bands."

Boone blew out a gust of breath. "Looks like I picked the wrong time to switch islands."

"This is Saba—we're a fortress! You'll be fine. You're staying with Gordon and Gerald, right?"

"The Double Gs, yes." When Sid snorted a laugh, Boone held up a hand. "Full disclosure, that one was Emily's."

"Of course it was."

"Your dad, is he going to be okay?"

"The wound wasn't bad. He's actually back at his desk, deploying the troops. We've got everything in hand, I think. Shelters are ready, curfew set, Royal Dutch Marines are in place. Nothing left to do, really. Some jackass decided to steal Mrs. Beach's car last night, a little yellow Hyundai Getz, but we'll deal with that after Irma. I'll actually be closing the annex here in a moment, if you feel like latching a few shutters."

"Happy to." Boone rose. "Any word on the missing boy?"

Sid went sober again. "No. And no sign of the kidnapper, either. He's probably gone to ground. One thing's for sure. With the port and airport closed, he's not going anywhere."

"Oh, bugger, I forgot my dry bag." Emily looked up from where she sat cross-legged on the floor, the Yorkipoo pup perched across a bare knee, contentedly chewing a plastic toy.

"Well, is there anything you really need in it?" Gerald asked.

"My GoPro is in there … I'd like to film during the storm. And Boone asked me to stick his ridiculously bright dive torch in there, and that might come in handy, yeah?"

"Well, it's only half past four. You've got plenty of time," Gordon said. "It's really just a waiting game, from this point forward."

"Right-o. Back in a jiff." Emily headed for the door, pausing to address the Double Gs' little dog, who had scampered after her. "And *you*, you little fuzzball, guard the house for me, yeah?"

The shadows were lengthening as she left the neighborhood behind the Saba Tourism office and turned left on The Road, walking past the Brigadoon pub. Nearly every cottage and store she passed was shuttered, as everyone hunkered down for the approaching hurricane. A light misting rain had begun, a refreshing tropical shower on any other day, but Emily suspected this was the outermost part of the storm.

The rental cottage was only a ten-minute walk from town and its red roof was soon in sight. Stepping off the road onto the sloping driveway, Emily immediately spotted a little yellow car parked off to the side. *Probably the landlord, making a last check of the property.* Emily had never seen Amber's car, since the landlord had always walked over, but with the drizzle it made sense she'd choose to drive today. She walked around the cottage to the door and spied a pair of hummingbirds hovering about.

"Aw, you're looking for your feeders, aren't you?" she said to the flitting little birds. "We'll have them back up, don't you worry. Now run along and find shelter!" A bleat rose from below and she spotted a pair of goats in a thicket of branches downslope from the cottage. "You too, goats!" *Where do animals go during a major storm?* she wondered, as she opened the door and entered the dark interior of the shuttered cottage. She realized she still had her sunglasses on. Not unusual—she typically wore them until sunset. Hooking them on the neckline of her tank top, she reached over to flip the light switch. Nothing happened. *Great. Storm's not even here and we've lost power.* Then it occurred to her that the landlord had probably come here to shut things off, knowing that Boone and Emily were sheltering elsewhere for the storm.

"Hey, Amber? You cut the power? I just forgot some stuff. You need a hand with anything?"

No answer. *Maybe she's in the cellar,* Emily thought, as she pulled out her smartphone and activated the flashlight function. She made her way to the bedroom and grabbed her dry bag. Returning, she found the door to the small, unfinished cellar and opened it, shining the light down the steps. "Amber? You down there? It's Emily." Silence. *Maybe she's out back,* she thought. She closed the door and turned.

There was a large shape blocking the hallway.

"Emily … that's a beautiful name." The voice was cold, matter-of-fact.

Although the phone's light wasn't directly on the man, there was enough illumination to know it was *him,* without a doubt. The man who had probably kidnapped that young couple. The man who might have killed someone on another island. The man she herself had seen a few days before. The coveralls, the hulking size.

Although Emily felt a wave of fear and adrenaline washing over her synapses, urging her to *RUN*, she kept her cool. The man was blocking the hall to both exits. Instead of screaming, she spoke.

"Oh thank God, you're here. The power's out. You're the handy-man, right? Amber said she was coming over any minute, so I thought that was *her* car, but it's yours, right?"

The man looked briefly confused by the burst of speech.

"Yes indeedy, Amber will be here any second but maybe you can get started, yeah? The fuse box is in the basement, I think." She reopened the door, but the man stepped closer and pushed it shut with a large hand.

"No." He reached for her.

Emily instantly knew she wasn't talking her way out of this. Remembering Sophie's mantra for Krav Maga—*whatever works*—she did several things in rapid succession: she screamed "Humming-goats!" figuring the non sequitur might confuse a synapse or two; tossed her flash-lit phone up towards the man's face, hoping he might instinctively grab for it—he did; and then kicked the man right in the balls. Her tennis shoe wasn't exactly a steel-toed boot and the man's coveralls were baggy, so the kick was by no means perfect, but he grunted in pain and staggered back. Emily dropped her dry bag and pushed past him, heading for the nearest exit, the back door in the kitchen. Bits of waning sunlight penetrated cracks in the shutters here and there and she managed to cross the kitchen, her fingers scrabbling for the knob. Just as they found it, an animalistic growl sounded from behind and a hand gripped her ponytail, yanking her head backward. *No, no, no, no—*

Her assailant pulled Emily back against him as a hard-muscled forearm wrapped around her throat, his other arm locking behind her head, clamping her carotid arteries into a vise. Emily's fear reached stratospheric levels—Sophie had showed her this very chokehold. *I've only got seconds before I pass out.* She twisted to the side, trying to apply pressure to the man's wrist, but his grip was like iron. Tiny spots of light began to swim in her vision. Fighting off panic, she switched tactics, slamming her heel down on the man's instep. The stomp was too far forward, smashing down on his toes. The man roared and lifted her tiny frame bodily from the ground, arching his back to hold her against his chest, the chokehold still locked in place.

Emily kicked her feet in the air, trying to reach the wall. *If I can just push off....*

But the sparkles on the edge of her vision suddenly became a flood.

Boone...!

Darkness took her.

22

At dusk, Boone stepped out of the rain and into the cottage. He was immediately greeted by Juniper, who jumped repeatedly at his side until he scooped her up, giving her a vigorous ear scratch. The sounds of chopping echoed from the kitchen and he made his way back to find Gordon and Gerald preparing dinner.

"Welcome back, young man," Gordon said. "What did Sid have to say?"

"Well, a few things, but the main takeaway was that we're likely in for a big one. Irma's a strong Cat 5 and coming right this way." He paused. "Where's Emily?"

"She went back for her dry bag." Gerald scooped a layer of diced onion onto his chef's knife and sent it into a pot on the stove. "She said she wanted her GoPro and some kind of dive light for the storm."

"Oh." He set the little puppy down. "When did she go?" The rain had picked up and it would be sunset soon.

"Right after you left," Gordon said, unscrewing the cap to the bottle of Saba Spice. "Care for a pre-hurricane tipple?"

"Not just now, thanks." *Something's wrong.* After helping Sid shutter the annex, Boone had decided to run by Sea Saba before returning. He'd heard they were quite good at reading the weather forecasts over there and figured a little extra information couldn't hurt. Boone had been gone for well over an hour—the walk to the rental cottage was only ten minutes.

"Are you all right, young man?"

Boone looked up. "I want to go get Emily," he said. "She should have been back by now."

"I'm sure she's all right," Gerald said. "Maybe she got caught in the rain. Tell you what—take my car. Keys are on the hook by the door."

"Thanks." Boone went straight for the keys and dashed out the door. The old Daihatsu started with a cough and he headed for The Road.

———◆◆◆———

The first thing Emily became aware of was a sound. A rattling sound, like BBs on a cookie pan. *No ... raindrops. Rain on metal.* She opened her eyes. She was lying on her side in the dirt, her cheek in a patch of mud. It looked like she was in some sort of floorless shack, the tin roof above explaining the sound. Apart from a broken chair, a couple plastic buckets, and a coil of nylon rope, the interior was empty. The shack was so ramshackle she was surprised it was standing, and she could see rain through gaps in the boards. A phrase entered her head, one that every damsel in distress seemed to utter when she came to, but there was no denying it was appropriate to the circumstances: *Where am I?* She decided to say the words out loud but all that came out was "Whrr mm mh?" If felt like there was some kind of cloth in her mouth, held in place by … *Oh, great, another cliché. He gagged me. No … not a gag.* Pushing out her upper lip, she looked down. *Duct tape. Well, we'll just see about that.* Emily tried to reach up to remove the tape … but no reach occurred. *Arms tied behind my back. Nice. And that probably means …* She tried to move her legs but felt resistance there, too. Looking at her feet, she saw her ankles were bound in layers and layers of duct tape. *Well, at least I'm not tied to railroad tracks.* Emily was shocked at how calm she felt. She immediately began flexing and twisting her wrists, testing the strength of the tape. *I wonder where tall, blond, and barmy is?*

Her mental query was quickly answered by nearby footsteps, squelching in the mud. Cursing and muttering floated in the air above the sounds of her captor's approach.

Think fast, Em. Try to interact with him? Or pretend I'm still out cold?

"I am coming, oh Great Ones! The Ascent will happen in time! But first I had to find a fucking walking stick because you let her break my fucking toe!"

Okayyyyy. Screaming at imaginary people, pissed at me for breaking his toe … fake unconsciousness it is. Emily closed her eyes and played possum.

Moments later, the man entered the shack and she could sense him sitting on the busted chair. A rustling sound, a thump as something flopped into the mud, a zipper being opened (*God, I hope that's not pants*), then the unmistakable sound of duct tape being pulled from a roll. *Oh, come on, I'm tied up enough already,* she protested to the universe. Risking a millimeter crack in an eyelid, she peeped through her eyelashes and saw with relief that the maniac was taping two of his toes together with half strips. *I got you good, you twat.* The thump she'd heard had been his boot, which he pulled onto his newly taped foot with a grunt of pain. Emily let her lids close as he finished lacing up. She heard him shift on the protesting chair and then her skin crawled as she felt rough fingertips brushing aside a loose lock of hair from her face.

"So beautiful. So like her." His voice was soft, surprisingly gentle, but then it *changed*, almost as if another person were speaking, and the hand quickly withdrew from her face. "No, of course not! I know! She belongs to you!"

Off his trolley, no doubt about it. But maybe I can use this. Listen and learn the looney lingo.

She felt his hands on her again and could tell he was preparing to lift her. It was surprising how much concentration it took to remain completely limp, but she did so, feeling her head loll as he sat her up, stood her up, then tossed her over his shoulder.

Crikey, someone hasn't had a bath in a while, she thought as her face met the back of his coveralls. *At least I can open my eyes now.* She watched the ground as they left the shack and entered the rain. The sun hadn't set and the raindrops on her back weren't heavy yet. She risked a slight turn of the head and saw lush, tropical greenery, the leaves flapping and branches bending in the growing wind. The shack stood in a cleared area in what looked to be a small banana plantation, the bananas the little cute ones she'd seen around the island. Something was bumping her head and she carefully tilted her head in the other direction. A large backpack over his other shoulder. *Jesus, how strong* is *this guy?* Even though Emily only weighed a hundred pounds dripping wet— which she actually *was* at the moment— a hundred pounds plus a backpack was still a *lot* to be hauling up a mountain. Looking back down, she saw they were on a steep trail. The trail soon gave way to stone steps, their rough-hewn surfaces pierced by plants and partially covered in moss and fallen leaves. *Oh, bloody hell, no,* Emily thought, as she finally divined the answer to her earlier damsel's query: "Where am I?" She slowly raised her head, looking down the steep steps, back the way they'd come. In the distance, a break in the rain clouds revealed a valley far, far below. Red roofs, like little miniatures at this distance, dotted the landscape. The Bottom. Then the clouds swallowed all. *Oh my God! He's taking me to the top of Mount Scenery.*

23

Boone knew something was wrong the second he pulled into the driveway. There wasn't any specific reason for the feeling; the cottage sat silent and shuttered, just as they had left it. It wasn't on fire, or anything. Nevertheless, there was that little prickle at the back of his scalp. He exited the car.

"Young man?" an elderly lady called out from the property next door. She was dressed in an orange poncho, flapping one side of it in a pseudo-wave. "Sorry to bother you, but I saw the car and thought Gordon or Gerald was here. Is Mrs. Beach okay?"

Beach ... Beach ... where have I heard that name? "I ... I'm sorry, ma'am, I don't know who you mean."

"Oh. Her car was here a couple hours ago, and it seemed very odd she'd be all the way over here, especially since the landlord closed the place up. She's got this little yellow thing, so I know it was hers."

"Did you see Mrs. Beach?"

"No, I'm sorry. By the time I got dressed to come over, the car was already heading toward Hell's Gate. But she lives in the hills above The Bottom, so that seemed strange."

"Well ... if she was here, maybe she was looking for the landlord, Ms. Linzey. She lives in Hell's Gate, doesn't she?"

"Oh, my goodness, yes. Thank you, I'll go give her a call. If the phones are still working, that is. Mine was acting up a little while ago."

The old lady headed back to her house and Boone made his way around the side to the little porch area. He pushed open the door to the cottage and stepped into the gloom, reaching for the switch by the entrance. Nothing happened when he flipped it.

"Emily! Em—" His voice caught as his eyes focused on something. The sun was almost set and the shuttered interior was quite dark. In the far room, near the door to the cellar, a bright light shone from the floor, illuminating a patch of ceiling. Boone rushed down the hall. *Emily's cell phone. And her dry bag.* "Emily!" he called again. *The cellar! Her stuff is right by the door, the lights are out.... Maybe she went to check the fuse, fell, hit her head.* Panic rose up inside as he grabbed her lit phone from the floor and tore the door open. He dashed down the cellar stairs. "Em! You here?" The cellar was full of the disassembled patio furniture he and Emily had brought in the day before. He flashed the light to and fro, then went to the fuse box. The switches had been flipped into the off position. He turned them back on. The cellar remained dark, but he saw lights come on upstairs. *Well, she's not down here. Her phone was up there by the door. If she'd fallen, she'd be right at the bottom of the stairs. No, something else happened.* He stuffed her phone into his pocket and raced back up the stairs, two at a time.

Boone stopped at the sight of Emily's dry bag. Picked it up. The prickly sensation returned. Suddenly his phone rang. He tore it from his pocket and looked at the screen. An unfamiliar number stared back at him. *Maybe it's her, calling from another phone!* He punched the talk button. "Em?"

"Uh, no. "R" maybe. Dis is Reynaldo. Boone, dat you?"

"I ... yes ... Reynaldo?"

"From Statia ... what, am I dat forgettable? Listen mon, I got info for ya."

"I ... yes, okay, sorry Reynaldo ... Rey .... I'm a bit distracted."

"Category 5 hurricane can do dat. So, listen up, hear? You wit me?"

Boone was back in the kitchen, now illumniated, looking around for any clue, anything that might ... "I'm sorry, Rey ... what? What do you have to tell me?"

"Da Quill. You were right. Dey found da Dutch girl up dere."

"What?"

"You told de police to search da Quill. Well, dey listened and found da missing girl, not far from a high point of da trail leading to da crater."

Boone paused in his frantic search, his eyes settling on a wall in the breakfast nook. "Murdered?"

"I'd say so. Her head was chopped clean off. Almost like what dey found in Kitts. Only dis time—"

The phone went silent for a moment, then an electronic bleep sounded, indicating a dropped call. Boone barely heard it as he continued to stare at the wall above the breakfast table. A calendar hung there, a beautiful Caribbean beach splashed above the month of September. Boone wasn't looking at the beach. He was looking at the white circle in the square for tomorrow, September 6. A full moon.

"No..." he whispered harshly. He yanked the calendar off its nail and looked at August, at the beginning of the month when

Imke De Wit had gone missing. *Reynaldo said it was a full moon the night before the man showed up looking to get to Saba. There! Full moon, August 7.* He went back another page. *The waitress on Saint Kitts went missing near the beginning of July. Full moon, July 9.* And, he remembered from the emailed files, the body had been found on July 10. The calendar fell from his fingers as his eyes lingered on a fan of brochures on the nook table. One declared Hike Mount Scenery! He grabbed it. *Kitts victim ... volcano. Statia ... volcano.* And now ... *Mount Scenery. It's a ritual.*

He raised his phone, locating Sid's number and punching the call button.

"We're sorry. All circuits are busy."

Boone scooped up Emily's dry bag and dashed for the door. The rain was coming down at an angle as the wind picked up. Boone raised his eyes toward Mount Scenery, but it was shrouded by fast-moving clouds in the twilit sky. He ran toward the little red car ... and stopped.

Yellow car. Mrs. Beach. Boone suddenly remembered. The stolen car Sid had mentioned. Boone was certain, now. *It's him. He took her. He took Emily.* Tears came to his eyes and panic began to bubble up inside. He savagely pushed it back down and focused. *He's taking her up to the summit. I know it. The stairs up the mountain are back in Windwardside ... but the neighbor said the car went the other way, toward Hell's Gate.* Then another memory marched front and center. Sid, telling them: *Now, there is a road, the Mountain Road, just past English Quarter—it takes you up to a spot in the main trail that lets you bypass the bottom quarter of the hike. But don't go asking for a certificate if you do that shortcut. That would be cheating!*

Boone ran to the Daihatsu, tossing Emily's dry bag onto the passenger seat and starting the car up as he juggled his phone, trying Sid again with no success. Then 911. Nothing. He pulled to the end of the driveway, mulling his options. The annex was closed, the police station all the way in The Bottom, a half hour in the other direction. Instinct guided his hand on the wheel as he swung to the right, heading for Hell's Gate. A minute later he slammed on the brakes. To his left, a road rose steeply up the side of the mountain. *Well, if that isn't a mountain road, I don't know what is.* He swung the car in a tight turn and gunned the engine, the little car doing surprisingly well on the significant incline.

Roadside foliage fluttered in the growing wind and rain pelted the windshield as Boone tore up the road in the waning glow of twilight. In minutes, he reached a dead end and skidded to a stop. Ahead ... a small yellow car. He dug through Emily's dry bag and extracted his dive light before leaping out of his vehicle and running toward the other car, its hatchback illuminated in the headlights of the Daihatsu. A Hyundai Getz. He flipped on the dive light and opened the hatch, peering inside. The rear seats had been lowered and a bright plastic object reflected the flashlight's glare. *Sunglasses. Lime green sunglasses. Emily!* To his right, a wooden signpost caught his eye. Next to it, a small boat on a trailer rusted away in the brush. Boone shined his light on the sign. A plank with *Ecolodge's Hotel Restaurant* crowned the post, with six arrowed signs below it. Five pointed to the left and only one pointed to the right: *Mt Scenery.* Boone didn't hesitate—he broke into a run.

———◆·◆———

Emily felt a tiny glimmer of triumph as she looked back down the stone steps. Her captor had produced a flashlight some time ago and a miniscule amount of its glow scattered behind, where Emily dangled over his shoulder like a sack of potatoes. The flash of lime green was visible for an instant before it was swallowed by the night. The item around her neck had slid down her inverted face as she bounced and jostled on her kidnapper's shoulder, but it had gotten stuck on her ponytail, requiring a toss of her head to free it. *Hopefully, that little stunt didn't alert Mister Cuckoo-bananas.*

"I know you're awake."

Bollocks. Still, she'd managed to leave a clue for Boone. *And he'll come for me. I know he will. But, on the off chance this dog's dinner isn't destined for a fairytale ending, I'll just have to rescue myself in the meantime.*

Again, Emily was gobsmacked she wasn't paralyzed by fear. Paralyzed by duct tape, yes … but her mind was sharp. *No sense blubbering and shivering from terror—that won't help me get out of this. Shivering from cold, on the other hand …* Emily wasn't exactly dressed for the occasion. Her clothing was more liquid than fabric at this point, the driving rain having soaked through her tank top and shorts. Rivulets of water streamed from her upside-down face.

"I said, I know you're awake."

Yeah, I heard you the first time, you stupid git. But you taped my mouth shut, so what do you want me to do, struggle and squirm? Oh, wait … I've got a better idea. Emily started humming a tune through the tape. Loudly. Specifically, the nursery song "Old Macdonald". *That song always drove me mum crazy; maybe it'll do the same for this berk.* Emily hummed with gusto, putting particular emphasis on the farm animal sounds, garbled and distorted through her tape gag.

"What are you doing?"

After a horse, cow, and rooster, she summoned a particular favorite, the pig. When she found she could do a pretty passable oink through the gag she burst into muffled laughter, dropping the song entirely and cycling through oinks, grunts, and squeals.

"What the *hell* are you doing?"

Psychological warfare for the illogical psycho, she thought. *And it sounds like I'm getting under his skin.* Emily didn't want to drive him into a murderous rage, but she thought she had some leeway. She had gathered from his periodic one-man conversations that he wouldn't harm her until they reached the summit, and maybe not even then, judging by some cryptic "at the appointed hour" rubbish he'd mumbled. She needed to slow him down and if she pushed his buttons enough, maybe he'd set her on the ground. *And if I can get him to free my mouth, then I can really get inside his head.*

Sure enough, all it took was about ten seconds of blessed silence, shattered by a rousing encore presentation of "Old Mac-Donald" and the man screamed, lowering her off his shoulder and sitting her on a rain-slick stone step. He shone a flashlight straight in her face.

"Stop it! Have you lost your mind?"

That gem of a question could have sent Emily into hysterical laughter, but instead she did her best not to squint, keeping her green eyes focused above the sphere of light. She spoke at length, her voice calm, collected ... and completely unintelligible.

"Nn, u hvn lh mmh mnd. Mmh sng-gng tu st sn."

A hand appeared in the glow of the flashlight. Rather than tearing the tape from her mouth, its removal was done with care.

"Again."

Emily spat out a wad of rag and took a moment to run her tongue over her lips. Mostly for her own benefit, but not entirely. *Anything I can do to distract, divert, delay.* "I said ... no, I haven't lost my mind. I'm singing to stay sane. You're taking us up a mountain and even if *you* don't rape me or kill me the storm surely will.

Well … the storm won't rape me. Just kill. But I digress. You *do* know there's a hurricane coming, right? Tonight? Like … a *big* hurricane?"

"How big?"

Good. Keep him talking. "A high Category 5, maybe the strongest this island has ever seen."

"Really?" His voice carried a touch of excitement. "I knew it was strong, but I haven't exactly kept up with the news. I've been … busy."

"Oh, I'll bet. Especially if you have to run around, doing errands for a Nazi smuggler. I mean, the sulphur mine is a *hike*, right?"

Silence. "How did you know about that?"

"Hey, you think you're the only one who has voices that tell them things?"

"Don't mock me! Don't mock *them!*"

Emily knew she was dancing on the edge, but she pushed ahead, nevertheless.

"I'm not! I'm not mocking you. When I saw you by the restaurant, I heard the voices. They … they told me to go to the sulphur mine. Could you … could you lower your torch a bit?"

The flashlight dropped to the side, no longer blinding her. "I saw you there," he said. "Above the mine."

"See? They must have known you would be there! *My* voices, I mean … not yours." *Easy, Em … think.* "The … the customs house."

"What…?"

"I was supposed to go there too. They told me to. The voices. Several nights ago. But then my dive shop made me go on a night dive instead. But I made them dive near the customs house." She lifted her green eyes to the shadowy face above her. "You were there, though. Weren't you?"

"Yes."

"I knew it," Emily said softly, allowing just a touch of huskiness to touch her voice. "I felt you up there."

More silence. "Perhaps ... there is a connection."

The mural down in Fort Bay popped into Emily's mind and she spoke in a whispered rush. "A symbiosis! Nothing in this universe exists alone."

The man looked at her sharply. "I know that phrase ... where do I...?"

"Perhaps your voices spoke it to you?" Emily quickly suggested.

The man was silent again, looking down at her. "The customs house. I would have chosen *you*, had you been there."

"Chosen me for what?"

"They haven't told you? Your voices?"

"I..." Suddenly, Emily felt her level-headed calm evaporate as the reality of her situation tore through her mind. *Oh my God, he's going to sacrifice me. He's going to take me to the top and kill me because he's batshit crazy and thinks something's telling him to—* She stomped down on the rising panic, cramming it back inside. "No ... no, they didn't tell me that part ... . I think I was supposed to learn from you...."

The man abruptly crouched, his face very close to hers. Emily had to admit, he was actually quite handsome ... for a murderous psychopath.

"Then I will teach you." He reached out a callused hand to brush aside the rain from her face.

Emily felt her gorge rise but she kept her eyes locked on his. "Yes ... teach me. Let me walk with you to the summit..."

But he was already lifting her, placing her back onto his shoulder. "I will teach you. So that you know just how *important* you are."

The wind howled as they resumed their climb into the darkness above. As her kidnapper shouted about volcanoes and the Earth, Emily firmly gripped the little rock she'd clawed from the ground behind her when he'd set her down, carefully securing it in her fingertips.

24

The steps were beginning to look like little waterfalls as Boone ran up them, taking them two at a time where he could. Although he was in peak physical condition, the footing was treacherous, and the driving rain, sometimes sheeting horizontally, made it difficult to see, even with the megawatt dive light. Three times he'd fallen, slipping on the mud and slick stones. His left knee ached from smashing it against a rock, but still he ran.

How long has he had her? How much of a head start? Boone kicked himself for not asking the neighbor when exactly the yellow car had left, but at the time he hadn't put two and two together, hadn't realized it was stolen. *What if he's already at the top? What if he's already—* A sob escaped his lips. *Stop it! He's probably carrying her. I* must *be gaining on them. Keep your eyes on the stairs ahead of you. No more falls.*

He almost missed it. A flash of green, lighter in hue than the wind-whipped plants that crowded the trail. He stopped abruptly, catching himself from taking another tumble, and swung the dive light onto the object. A whistle! The green whistle on its lanyard, the one Gordon had given her. *Better than a bread crumb,* he thought, scooping it up and stuffing it into a pocket. Of course, the killer might have found it on her ... tossed it aside. *Shut up! Run!*

Ahead, rudimentary metal banisters began appearing. Many were incomplete, just support poles jutting from beside the steps, but wherever a railing was fully in place, Boone grabbed hold and pulled himself up the mountain at greater speeds. After what seemed like an eternity, but was probably on the order of minutes, Boone reached a fork in the trail beside a tiny roofed shelter with a bench inside. Across from the shelter, a sign for Bud's Mountain pointed ahead and to the left. The terrain was flatter here, devoid of steps, and Boone flashed his light across the muddy ground. *Boot prints. Deep ones, so he's carrying a lot of weight.* Boone took the fork to the right and dashed up the trail.

As he reached a bit of a bowl in the terrain, Boone paused, gulping in lungfuls of humid air. The wind swirled here, and he was somewhat shielded from the rain by the thickening of the foliage around him. Strange, moss-laden trees surrounded him and huge ferns that looked like something out of a prehistoric diorama dotted the landscape. Weird moss balls, like alien pods, hung from nearby branches, their bulbous shapes swinging in the wind. *I read about this ... what was it called? The elfin cloud forest. Must be near the top.*

A sudden cry jolted his heart and he swung his dive light into the trees to the right of the trail. *It sounded like a scream, but ... weird.* As he heard it again, he realized what it was and his suspicions were confirmed when his light found the source: a goat. It blinked its vertical pupils in the blinding light, then bounded away into the trees.

Something else danced at the edge of his peripheral vision and he swung his head back to a spot above the trail. Peering up into the darkness, he squinted through the rain. *Did I see something?* He ran a few more steps, looking for a better angle. *There!* In the distance was a steep set of steps and above, a light flashed between the trees before being swallowed up in the rain and dark.

Boone launched himself up the trail.

"So … let me get this straight…" Emily said. She was sitting in a puddle beside the trail next to a pair of arrowed signs. They both said *Scenic View* and they pointed in opposite directions. "If you make the sacrifice at the top of a volcano, the volcano will erupt?"

"Not just one … *all* of them … but I need to awaken one to begin the cycle." The man was shining his light on a water-logged map that fluttered dangerously in the wind. For the third time, he aimed the beam at the signs with their contradictory arrows, then returned with frustration to his map.

Behind her back, Emily felt the duct tape tear again as the little piece of rock she'd palmed bit into the material. For the previous half hour, perched atop her captor's shoulder with her arms behind her back, she'd had free reign to scrape at her restraints as the man concentrated on the strenuous work of hauling her up the slippery steps, all the while spewing a mad monologue of his beliefs and desires. *Seems like he's got a chubby for volcano-induced End Times*, she thought, feeling the edge of the rock tear another few strands of tape.

"Which one…?" the man muttered angrily.

Emily was certain that with one good yank she could tear her wrists free. This momentary confusion—two summits this lunatic

"Well … that seems … on the nose." *Shut up, Emily!* But the man didn't appear to have heard her. "Listen, what happens to you? After?"

"What do you mean?"

"Well, let's say you … do … whatever you do … to me…" She forced herself to go on. "And the volcano goes: 'Good job, Aidan! Boom!' What happens to you?"

Aidan smiled, the hesitation of a moment before vanishing as he spoke with quiet fervor. "I will Ascend and become one with those I serve."

"Yyyyeah, okay, but what if it *doesn't* happen? Like those other times you told me about? You're on top of a mountain with a Category 5 hurricane coming. You're going to be killed."

"No. The building under the communications tower is concrete. If the ritual does not bring about The Great Awakening, I will shelter there and wait for the storm to pass."

"What if it's locked?"

The man patted a side pocket of his coveralls. "Prybar."

"Oh … well, you're prepared."

"I have many tools," he said, setting his flashlight down beside Emily and reaching for the backpack he'd dropped beside the trail.

Unzipping it, he withdrew a machete and Emily's heart rose into her throat. She felt her body start to tremble, out of her control. The handle was wrapped in duct tape. *It fixes everything!* her mind crowed. The blade was almost black, scratched and pitted in places, but one area where it had clearly been cared for was the edge. It *gleamed*.

"You won't feel any pain," he said softly. "It's all been a learning experience for me, but I know how to do it properly, now. When a volcano erupts, the top is removed, and the lava and ash … the blood and breath … flow from the rupture. So, too, with you."

He spoke as if this were a comfort and Emily finally lost her composure, tears streaming from her eyes, joining the rain on her cheeks. It was now or never. She glanced at his open backpack, spying the tops of several plastic water bottles. "I'm thirsty," she sobbed. "I don't want to die thirsty."

"Of course. You have earned this kindness ... Em." He thrust the tip of the machete into the wet earth behind him and turned for the backpack.

Fear shrieking in her thoughts, Emily tried Boone's trick of slowing the breath, focusing on each inhalation and exhalation, and then snaked a hand from behind her back as Aidan dug through the backpack. When he turned back to face her, a water bottle in his hand, she struck!

The flashlight wasn't the heavy kind the police carried, but it had some heft. Snatching it from the mud, she swung it against Aidan's temple as hard as she could and the man grunted, falling back on the muddy trail with a splat. She brought her other hand around to above her ankles, the piece of rock held firmly, viciously digging at the little vee she'd begun in the duct tape. Emily watched with terror as Aidan rose to his hands and knees, mere inches from the machete. Savagely ripping at her bonds, she winced as she slipped and cut her calf. With superhuman effort, she grabbed hold and tore the gash in the tape apart, leaping to her feet ... and nearly pitching onto her face as pins and needles erupted in her newly freed legs.

"*You ... BITCH!*" The dark shape rose.

Emily staggered into the driving wind and rain, running toward the tower.

"You ... BITCH!"

Boone heard the savage voice as he reached the top of the stairs. He hurtled up the trail, spotting a flashlight on the ground. A dark shape was rising from beside it, something metallic in its hand catching the light. Dousing his own flashlight, Boone suddenly realized just how dark it had become as the wind began to howl through the thick branches of the cloud forest. Keeping his eyes on the spot of light ahead, he ran, wincing at the pain in his knee from one of his earlier tumbles. The panic he felt for Emily was still there, but he calmed it. *He just yelled at her, so she's probably still alive.* But from the rage he'd heard in the man's voice, that might be a temporary condition if he didn't act fast.

The man was moving away, presumably after Emily, and Boone ran toward him, quickly sifting through his options. First: get him to stop chasing Emily. Then: take away his weapon. He gained on the bobbing flashlight, then shouted. "Hey! You!"

The light stopped. The outline of the broad-shouldered man turned. Boone could make out the weapon, now. A machete. *Or cutlass, as Sid's dad would likely say,* Boone thought. The same weapon that had decapitated those victims on the other islands. The flashlight swung up to focus on Boone, illuminating the fat drops of rain that fell from Irma's outermost bands. The light began to move toward him.

"I know you," the voice said, raised to be heard over the wind.

All at once, Boone's course of action clicked into place. He reached up to his throat. "And I know *you.* Imke de Wit sent me." He grasped the blue bead and tore the cord from his neck. "She wants me to give you this." He held the cord up, the bead hanging from it in the beam of light. The flashlight's advance halted and Boone tossed the necklace at the man's feet. The man started to aim his light at it and Boone swung his own dive light up and flicked it on.

Emily had been right about how ridiculously bright the thing was, and its sudden ignition was blinding, forcing the man to raise an arm to shield his eyes. Fortunately for Boone, it was the arm with the machete. Boone didn't risk a capoeira tumble to close the distance, not in this soup of mud and moss. He simply dashed forward, dropping his light at the last moment as he hurled himself on the man, his large hands gripping the man's arm and applying a wrist-lock. Boone's skills in Brazilian Jiu-jitsu weren't as showy as what he used in capoeira, but they were extremely effective. He planned to simply snap the man's wrist, but when he began the maneuver, forcefully applying the pressure, it was like trying to bend an iron bar. His opponent dropped his flashlight as well, reaching for one of Boone's own wrists. Boone twisted, keeping his grip out of the man's reach.

In the glow of the fallen flashlights, Boone assessed his foe. Even in baggy coveralls, it was clear he was extremely muscular. He was making horrible, rage-fueled sounds, almost a gargling in his throat, as he fought to free his machete arm. That arm was corded in muscle, straining to resist the wrist lock. The man kicked out a boot, catching Boone on a bare shin with a glancing blow. With a supreme effort, Boone threw his body weight onto the inverted arm and finally the man released the machete. It landed with a splash in a nearby puddle.

Boone's triumph was short-lived, as his full-body effort to force the disarm had thrown him off balance and the man finally got a hold of him. A callused hand grabbed Boone by the throat, forcing him to release the man's wrist. *His strength is insane!* Boone thought as the fingers tightened on his neck, realizing that madness probably *did* play some part in how powerful he was. Before his opponent could bring his other hand into play, Boone snapped a knee up into the man's sternum. White light seared his vision, as he realized he'd used his injured knee, and the blow had minimal effect. Resorting to a move frowned upon in capoeira tournaments, Boone executed a *telefone*, or telephone, clapping both palms against the man's ears and sending a burst of air pressure into the man's ear canals, causing sudden pain, maybe even rupturing the eardrums, if he was lucky.

The man screamed in agony, losing his grip on Boone's throat. Boone snapped a quick *bênção*, or blessing kick at the man's chest to drive him back, the simple frontal kick meant to give him some breathing room.

Boone hadn't yet seen Emily and started to call out for her, but stopped himself. *No. She may be hiding. Or trying to get around us, back to the steps.* He didn't want her to give herself away, so Boone instead focused on the task at hand. *Time to finish this,* he thought, taking two *ginga* steps and swinging a simple *martelo*—a hammer kick up toward the man's temple. To his surprise, his target was shielded, as the killer whipped his arm up in an efficient block. *Wonderful. Not only is he strong, but he has training.* Boone decided to risk the kick he'd shown off to Sophie. He'd once used it in Bonaire to drop a man who was menacing a friend with a knife, but hadn't used it in an actual fight since, as it had resulted in a fracture of his opponent's skull. *But if that happens this time, I'll go on to live a long and carefree life.*

Capoeira's famous *meia lua de compasso*, or compass half-moon kick, was probably not something his opponent had seen, and if you were unprepared for its unorthodox delivery, it could end you. The muddy trail was saturated, so Boone decided to fake a slip, falling back toward a firmer section of ground he'd felt in his *ginga* footwork, planting his hands firmly on the ground beneath his legs and hunching over. The man moved in, looking for his own quick victory. Boone continued his motion, turning it into a low spin, sweeping his outer leg and whipping it up and across at blinding speed.

It might have been a perfect kick. *If.* If the ground hadn't been so slick and his supporting foot hadn't slipped. If he had been fighting barefoot, in his accustomed manner. If his knee wasn't screaming at him. The kick went high and Boone tried to regain his balance, preparing to tumble away with an *aú* cartwheel, but a low whoosh heralded the arrival of his opponent's fist, smashing into the side of Boone's head. He turned with the blow, staggering away in a sloppy spin as his ears rang from the impact. He cartwheeled back further, nearly falling, dizzy from the blow. *If I hadn't rolled with that punch, he would've taken my head off,* Boone thought, then realized the man was crouching down for some reason. Seeing an opportunity, Boone advanced, lining up for another attack.

"Boone! Look out!"

Emily? Thank God— But Boone suddenly realized why the man had crouched as a gleam of metal caught the light of a fallen flashlight. He barely had time to leap back as the machete blade whipped through the air, the curve near its tip striking a rib before sliding across his flank, slicing a shallow gash in his skin. Boone continued to retreat, knowing he'd narrowly escaped disembowelment.

The lunatic charged, madness shining in his eyes as sheets of rain flew horizontally across his path. Preparing to dodge and counterattack, Boone took two steps back … but only one of those steps met with the ground. In the driving rain and darkness, he hadn't realized he'd left the trail and had been on the edge of a ravine.

"BOONE!"

Emily's scream receded into the howling wind as Boone pitched backward and fell from the cliff.

25

The Servant roared with triumph. How fitting that the mountain itself would claim the interloper. Another cry from his Chosen drew his attention back toward the communications tower. It was too dark, the rain too heavy, to see her. *But she is there, and there is nowhere to go.* He turned and went for his flashlight but paused, looking at the one his opponent had dropped. It was much brighter than the one the Servant had brought, and he claimed his spoils of war, returning with it to the edge where his foe had fallen.

Shining the powerful beam down into the ravine, he searched for any sign of the tall man, but the rain and swirling mists kept the light from reaching very far. He knew his instrument had struck home, tasting flesh. If it was a deep cut, the fool would bleed out ... if he wasn't already dead, smashed on a rock somewhere down below.

Forget him! a voice from within said. *He is done for, and you still have work to do. Though you cannot see it, the moon is full and the time is right!*

"But, where shall I perform the ritual?" he asked those he served, remembering he had never settled the issue of where the summit was.

It matters not. This whole mountaintop is your altar. Now ... find her.

The Servant headed toward where he had heard the girl cry out, Boone's dive light in one hand and the machete gripped tightly in the other.

———◆◆———

No, no, no, no ... he can't be dead. Boone! Emily wept as the scene kept playing over and over in her head: the sickening *thunk* as the machete struck his side ... the pools of light from the two flashlights catching his long arms flailing at the rain-filled air as he fell backward and vanished over the edge.

Now, a light was moving, headed toward her. She was crouched beside the yellow building at the base of the communications tower and she quickly ducked around the side of the building. The door on the side facing the trail had been locked and she'd been looking for another way in, when the sounds of the fight had drawn her back toward the trail. A sob rose in her throat and escaped her lips.

Stop! You've got to be quiet now. She looked again at the building, debating going all the way around to see if there was another door or a window, but she realized that if she got inside, all she'd be doing would be trapping herself. *You have mobility. You can outrun him. You can escape around him, get to the stairs.* She peeked around the corner. The light was swinging to and fro as Aidan searched for her.

No ... I can't run. Boone may still be alive. I have to hide ... evade. If I can get around him, maybe I can get back to where Boone fell. The other light will still be on the trail; it should be near there. Glancing toward the back of the building, she spotted a metal ladder leaned against the side. An idea bloomed and she dashed for the ladder, climbing quickly to the roof of the blockhouse that served as the base of the massive tower. Looking up through the rain, mists, and dark, she could only see a short way into the internal cat-walks and ladders that ran up its spine. The steel girders creaked and moaned above her head and a gust of wind staggered her, blowing her ponytail horizontal. *Climbing up that would be very dangerous in these winds,* she thought. But she did so anyway. Just enough so that she could see the approaching flashlight.

"Hey! Hey, you barmy bastard!" she yelled, competing with the shrieking wind, and gripping the rungs tightly to keep from being blown off.

The light swung up and found her.

"Lot of trouble getting me up the mountain, yeah?" she shouted at the top of her lungs, all the while thinking through the mad ravings he'd shared with her on their trek up the steps. "And you timed it for those voices, didn't you? The 'appointed hour,' blah, blah, blah. Too bad I'm gonna cock it all up for you. I bet your little volcano worship codswallop won't work if I kill *myself* before you chop my noggin off. I'm gonna climb to the top and jump!"

"You won't do it," the man shouted. "Come down from there before you hurt yourself."

"Oh, yeah, I wouldn't want to slip and *chop my head off!*"

"Come down from there! Emily! Come down." The flashlight swung around the base of the building as he searched for how she'd gotten up there. It tilted back up at her. "You must ... you must fulfill your purpose!"

She couldn't see his face and it was hard to detect nuance in a shout, but she thought he might be wavering. "Why don't *you* fulfill it? You got a hard-on for apocalypse, why don't you just *choose* yourself!"

There was a pause. "That's not..." Aidan's voice trailed off. Another pause, then some muttering that Emily couldn't pick out from the howl of the wind. Then, his voice returned, full of renewed purpose. "No! It must be you! It *will* be you!"

"You want me? Come get me, you twat! You killed my man ... I have nothing left to live for!" She then made a show of climbing higher.

"No!" the man roared, dashing toward the building, his flashlight vanishing below the roofline.

Emily immediately scampered back down the tower, dashing across the roof to the side furthest from the ladder that led to the ground. She sat her butt on the edge of the roof, squinting through the rain into the darkness. Far in the distance, a glow. *The other torch. That's where Boone fell.* Emily looked down. She couldn't see the ground in the pitch black, but the roof wasn't very high and with all the rain, the mud would soften her fall. Grabbing hold and twisting around, she dangled her bare legs into the night air, locking her eyes on the spot across the roof where Aidan would climb up. She didn't have to wait long as a bright light illuminated the top of the ladder and she could make out the sounds of a rapid ascent, as his boots clanged on the rungs. She let go, dropping through the rain, her green tennis shoes burying themselves in the muck.

Emily dashed for a nearby tree, slipping behind it and looking back at the building. A bright light was now climbing the tower above the roof, just as she'd hoped. *The wind and rain and clouds ...*

even with a light he can't see very far. He thinks I'm higher up! Turning back toward the distant glow on the trail, she broke into a run.

◆ ◆

Meh!! Wind. Rain. *MEHHHHH!!*

"Jesus…!" Boone came to with a jolt as something licked his cheek. His sudden movement startled the little goat and it bounded away through the brush. He sat up, wincing, trying to decide which hurt more, the sharp pain at his side or the dull pain in his head. *I hit my head on a tree or something when I fell … managed to grab hold of a root before I blacked out.* This recollection came to him as a fuzzy near-dream. The wind was howling around him, moaning through the trees. He was lying in a thick stand of leaves and water-logged moss—the lush foliage of Mount Scenery likely having saved his life. *Helps that this wasn't actually a cliff … more like a steep slope.*

Emily!

Urgency flushed the woozy lethargy from his brain and he immediately began to climb, ignoring the aches and pains as he clawed his way from root to trunk to rock. *How far did I fall?* In the dark, the rain sheeting down, it was impossible to see very far. He paused, digging into the pockets of his shorts for either his or Emily's phone. His fingers found one, and as they closed around it, he became aware of something in the pocket below it, one of the outer cargo pockets he almost never used. Boone had a flash of memory of the one time he'd put his wallet in there by accident and hadn't found it for days. Dragging the phone out, he turned on its flashlight feature and retrieved the object.

Chad's chainmail glove. Why is…? Boone suddenly remembered: after that lionfish hunt gone wrong, he'd found it under a bench while preparing the boat for storage. *I shoved it in that outer pocket and completely forgot about it.* Tucking it back into the pocket, he raised the little phone light above his head, trying to see the top.

"Oh, thank God, thank God! I thought you … Boone!" The voice from above had begun as a harsh whisper but emotion pushed stealth aside as Emily cried out.

"Emily! Are you all right?"

"Asked the man who fell off a cliff." A flashlight shone down, and Emily's voice spoke beside it. "Looks like that nutter took your torch—this one's his. Are you hurt? Can you make it up?"

"Yes … to both…" Boone grunted. He was happy to see he wasn't far from the top, and knowing Emily was alive reinvigorated his muscles. "The killer … is he?"

"I've sent him on a wild goose chase…or … goose *climb*. But I don't know how long it'll take before he catches on."

"Well … it'll take me a while to get up there, so go hide until—"

"Oh, sod off, Prince Charming, I'm not going anywhere. Loony McLoonface had a bunch of goodies in his backpack. Here." A length of nylon rope smacked Boone in the face. "Woulda tossed it sooner but I had to tie it off."

Boone pocketed the phone and grabbed hold, hauling himself along the line. "Have I mentioned that I love you?"

"Oh, a bunch of rope gets you going, eh? I had no idea you were into that. Now quit fannying around and get your arse up here so we can go back down the mountain."

Boone thought as he climbed. Beside him, a little river of water sluiced down the slope above, carving out a trench in the mud. "These winds are just the outer bands … it won't be long before we get hit with the heavy stuff."

"How long?"

"I don't know. But if we try to get back down the mountain, I don't think we'll make it. The steps will be waterfalls by now. Also … Em, I gotta be honest … I'm … I'm not feeling my best."

There was a hitch in Emily's voice as she spoke. "We'll make it, Boone. There's a concrete building under the tower. We can shelter in there."

Boone neared the top and Emily's hand reached down and clasped his wrist, helping to haul him the rest of the way up. He threw his arms around her, hugging her tight. "Thank you, Em."

Emily gripped him tightly, speaking into his chest. "Thank *you*. For coming for me. I knew you would."

"Always." Boone spoke into her rain-soaked hair. "Though you seemed to be doing just fine without me."

"Yeah, well, let's revisit that thought if we get out of this alive." She stopped as she became aware of something wet pressing against her. It didn't feel like rain. It was warm. She stepped back from their embrace, shining her light on Boone's side. There was blood. A lot of it. "Jesus, Boone."

"It's not as bad as it looks but … like I said, I think a hurricane-hike down the mountain is out of the question for me."

"Okay. The building then." She grabbed her captor's backpack and took Boone by the arm, guiding him back toward the communications tower. "Now, I think, between the two of us, we can barricade ourselves in, keep Aidan out…"

"Aidan?"

"His name. Means fire. Never mind." She stopped suddenly, dousing the flashlight.

"What is it?"

"Shh!" she hissed, reaching up to grab Boone by the hair and pull his ear down to her mouth. "I had him climbing the radio tower," she whispered. "Made him think I was going to jump from the top. But I don't see his light now."

Boone stuck his hand in a pocket, searching. "Maybe a gust of wind got him," he said in a low voice. "Remember, the higher you are, the stronger the wind." He unclipped his sandals, kicking them aside. His bare feet felt more secure in the muddy terrain.

"It doesn't matter. We need to get out of the storm." She grabbed his arm, hurrying him toward the building. She kept her light doused, but the red lights of the tower told her where to go. "There's a locked door on this side. Might be another way in around back—I didn't have time to check."

"Head for the door," Boone said in a low voice. He thought he'd seen movement. Maybe just a tree limb swaying in the wind. *But maybe not.*

———— ◆ ⋅ ◆ ————

The Servant crouched in a clump of tropical bushes beside an old satellite dish, mere yards from the entrance to the building beneath the communications tower, waiting for his prey to come to him.

He had acted out of panic before. The girl had seemed sincere in her threat to kill herself and he had climbed nearly a hundred feet before doubt set in. After a particularly strong gust of wind had blown aside the rain and mist above him—nearly blowing him off the ladder as well—he was able to see that the Chosen was not on the tower. Realizing he'd been had, he'd scrambled back down to the roof, dousing the dive light and waiting for the voices to tell him what to do.

Rather than speak, they *showed*: the other flashlight, his own, moving about down the trail. Climbing down the wall-side ladder, he moved into the foliage, planning to flank the trail and beat them to the steps. He had halted when he realized they were headed this way.

They seek shelter, the voices whispered. *Let them come to you.*

And so he had, letting his eyes adjust to the darkness, keeping a healthy amount of tropical leaves between himself and the approaching light. After a moment, the light was doused.

Patience.

Now, shadows approached as his quarry reached the building. The Servant shifted on his haunches, tightening his grip on the hilt of the machete.

"Flick your light on, just for a second," the tall man said. The light came on, spotlighting the padlock on the door. The girl had the Servant's backpack and dropped it to the side as her companion tested the door. "The door's internal lock is open, but this padlock ... I could probably break that locking plate off."

"There's a window over here," the Chosen said, swinging her light to the right of the door.

"Looks like it's one of those fixed types, like on warehouses. Think we'll have better luck with the door. Lose the light."

The sound of the wind and rain masked the Servant's movement as he slipped around behind the pair, raising the machete. He would take the Chosen to the rooftop and sacrifice her there. But first ... to dispose of this *rival*. The couple were just dark shapes in the storm, but the tall man's lanky frame was clear enough. The Servant charged, swinging the blade in a downward arc just as the shape spun around, raising a hand.

The machete came to a jarring halt.

◆·◆·◆

With the sound of the storm drowning out everything else, Boone had felt the man's advance more than he'd heard it. On the approach to the communications tower, he'd slipped Chad's chainmail glove onto his left hand. As Emily flicked off the flashlight, the hair on the back of his neck had stood on end and he'd turned his head to the side, spotting the flash of movement. Spinning around, he stepped into his attacker, catching the machete low on the blade in his gauntleted grip. He felt the heavy weapon bite into the stainless steel links, jarring the bones in his hand, but he grabbed hold and held the blade tight as he cocked his leg and snapped a kick into the man's stomach. Nothing flashy, nothing fancy, just a hard and fast sidekick. As his foot made contact, he yanked the machete, pulling it free from the man's grip. Hurling the crude weapon as hard as he could, he sent it spinning into the night, the damaged chainmail glove flying off after it.

Emily flicked the light back on, shining it in Aidan's face. Boone attacked, spinning an *armada* kick at the killer's temple. It was a glancing blow and the man screamed in rage as he hurled himself at Boone, driving his head into Boone's midsection. Boone grappled with him, trying to break free from the lunatic's enormous strength. His opponent shot out a hand and gripped his throat.

I'm too slow, Boone thought frantically. *That cut may have been deeper than I thought.*

"Yaaa!" A shrill cry pierced the wind as Emily kicked the heel of her foot against the side of the man's knee joint. Something gave and the man shrieked, swinging his left arm at her. The kick had brought her too close and Emily's head rocked to the side as the killer backhanded her, catching her on the cheekbone. The flashlight slipped from nerveless fingers as she wobbled on unsteady legs. Stumbling three or four steps away, she sat down hard in the mud, stunned.

Boone screamed in a primal fury, his neck cords bulging against the choking grip on his throat. Grabbing hold of the arm with both hands, he kicked his legs up, clamping them on that arm's shoulder as he torqued his entire body, spinning the man to the muddy ground with a splash as he combined a capoeira take-down with a jiu-jitsu scissor lock. At the moment of impact, he twisted his grip with all his might and this time the man's arm popped, dislocating at the shoulder and snapping at the elbow. Boone moved to finish him off, but his opponent was so mad-dened by rage and pain that he lashed out with his good arm, his fingers searching for—and finding—the machete cut in Boone's flank. The man dug his fingers into the wound and Boone felt all the strength leave him as a wave of nausea washed over him, his skin growing cold and clammy. His grip on the killer fell away.

Useless arm dangling, Aidan straddled Boone, once more clamp-ing an iron grip on Boone's throat with his good hand. "I've just decided," the man spat through clenched teeth as he squeezed. "I'll sacrifice *you*, too. A pair, one male, one female, it's perfect! *This* time it will happen! *This* time, the Earth will *awugggh*—"

He was cut off mid-sentence by a heavy thudding sound and his head pitched to the side. Emily stood behind him, a fist-sized rock in her hand. She swung it against his head again, and Aidan swayed, eyes rolling up, before toppling to the side into a puddle.

"Told you ... rock beats ... everything..." Emily gasped between breaths. She had a cut inside her cheek from the man's punch and she spat blood into the mud, tossing the rock aside with a splash before helping Boone crawl out from under the killer. "As they say in Krav Maga ... *whatever works*. I think Sophie would be proud."

"I know *I* am," Boone said, gulping air and wincing from the pain in his side. It was taking every ounce of concentration to keep from passing out. "Is he dead?"

"I dunno," she said. "Would kinda make things easy if he was…" Just then a sizeable branch snapped with an explosive *crack* and spun away in the near distance. "Boone, we've got to get inside. Check his pockets. He said something about a pry bar. I'll see if he's got a pulse."

Boone quickly found a foot-long prybar in a side pocket of the coveralls and slid it free. "Got it."

Emily lifted her fingers from the man's throat. "He's alive. Hoo-fucking-ray. So, what do we…?"

"Well … I'm not a murderer. And neither are you."

"No. But…"

"But just because we won't kill him doesn't mean we've got to drag his batshit-crazy ass into shelter with us. Leave him to the storm."

"Fine by me, but how do we make sure he … oh! Oh, *hells*, yes!" Emily scrambled for the fallen flashlight and skidded to her knees beside the backpack.

"What?"

She held a roll of duct tape aloft. "Allow me to introduce the wonder of the ages. I'm intimately acquainted with *this* little roll of joy." She advanced on the fallen killer.

"You want me to—" Boone began.

"Oh, no, no, nooooo. *I've* got this. You get that door open." She knelt in the mud beside Aidan. "Sauce for the goose, you daft prat," she snarled, tearing loose a long strip of tape. "You're the gander, in case your volcano gods don't do idioms." She wrapped the man's arms together behind his back, sparing no expense. A loud ping sounded from behind.

"Got the … got the door…"

"Good. Almost done with this tosser," she spat, trussing his ankles in a mummy's wrap of duct tape. She rolled him faceup so he wouldn't drown in the growing puddles. "Hey Boone, should we drag him—"

A loud splash cut her off and she snatched the flashlight from the ground and swung it toward the door. Boone lay on his back in the mud.

"Boone!" Emily slipped in her rush to reach him, faceplanting in a puddle. Staggering to her feet, she closed the distance and threw herself down beside him. His side was soaked with blood, far more than before. She shook him. "Boone…?"

"Martin's made pumpkin *sopa*…" Boone slurred.

He's hallucinating about his cook friend back in Bonaire, Emily thought. Tears warred with the rain sluicing down her face. "You betcha, Booney. And Martin's got some of those *pastechi* belly bombs you like so much, too." She moved behind his head and knelt, sitting him up so she could get her hands under his shoulders. "Let's go have some, yeah? Gonna need your help, though, 'kay? You've got a foot and a half of height on me and you wouldn't want me pulling a muscle dragging you, now would you?"

"No … never…"

"Okay then. Upsy daisy…" Emily managed to get Boone onto his feet, draping him over her shoulder while maintaining a grip on the flashlight. "Jesus, Boone," she grunted, "how many of those soursop smoothies have you been snarfing down?" Staggering toward the door, she pulled it open and lugged Boone inside.

Aside from some red and green buttons that glowed from a back room, the building beneath the tower was pitch black. The place appeared to be divided into sections and she sat him down against an interior wall. "Boone … you with me?"

He moaned softly but made no intelligible reply.

Emily lightly slapped his face, then planted her mouth on his, pressing a kiss against his lips.

Boone blinked, seeing her. "Em…?"

That did the trick. No surprise there. Emily reached down, pulled his bloody shirt over his head, and wadded it up. She briefly suppressed an unexpected snicker as she spied the pink whistle on a lanyard on his neck, the other one the Double Gs had given them. One look at the blood on his side and the brief spark of levity was extinguished. "Boone, I need you to do something for me, okay? Here." She stuffed the shirt into his hands and pressed the mass of cloth over the wound. "Press this tight, yeah?"

Boone winced, roused by the pain, and nodded vigorously.

"Back in a jiff!" Emily ran back outside. She spared a moment to flick the light toward her former captor. Duct tape shone in the light and she felt a touch of satisfaction. A loud crash sounded nearby, as something blew loose from the communications tower and struck the ground a few feet away from her. *Here comes Irma.* Emily grabbed the tape and the backpack and went back inside, pulling the door closed. Outside, the wind keened and moaned. She dashed back to Boone's side. Her flashlight caught his face, and she was relieved to see his color was improved.

"How … how's our friend?" he asked.

"Still communing with the mud and coated in duct tape." She dug a bottle of water out of the backpack and unscrewed the cap. "How you doing? Looking a bit less zonked, if you ask me."

"Better … I think. Em … if we don't … if…"

"You 'bout to get maudlin? Shut your piehole and drink this." She pressed the mouth of the bottle to his lips. He took it with his free hand. While he was busy with that, she gently pried his other hand and the blood-soaked shirt loose from his side, shining her light on the gash along his flank. She shuddered, then reached into the backpack for another bottle and poured part of the contents onto the blood that obscured the wound.

"Cold."

"Yeah, I bet. We'll do something about that in a moment, Booney-boy." She stripped off her sodden tank top, catching a little glint in his eyes as she did so. "Don't get any ideas. This is for the good of medical science."

"Your sports bra ... isn't green," Boone said. "I must be delirious."

"Hey, sometimes I like yellow. Now shut up and let Doctor Emily concentrate."

She folded the tank top into fourths, then rinsed the wound again. Pressing the square of wet cloth over the cut with one hand, she retrieved the dwindling roll of duct tape with the other, tearing off strips with her teeth and affixing the makeshift bandage over the wound. "Like they say, duct tape fixes everything!"

Boone laughed out loud, the laugh turning into a grimace. "Ease up on the comedy, Em ... I think that machete broke a rib."

"Right-o, I'll dial it back ... but it's so hard, when I'm—" A loud bang cut her off, as something crashed against the concrete building. "Bloody hell..."

"How fast ... were the winds ... when you..."

"Well, the last time I checked before Volcano-lover knocked my ass out and dragged me up a mountain ... almost 180 miles per hour near the eye." The door rattled as the winds outside clawed at it. Emily headed over to it. "Lucky for us they didn't throw this deadbolt, yeah? But now we need to keep out the wind and lunatics, so..." She tried the lock. It didn't budge. She tried again. "Bloody hell," she grunted. "Rusted. No wonder they left it ... there!" With a supreme effort, she managed to turn the knob, locking the bolt in place. "Mum always had me open the pickle

26

As Hurricane Irma approached the Northern Leewards, she was so powerful that her winds registered on seismic instruments designed to detect earthquakes located over 200 miles away on the French island of Guadeloupe.Just before one a.m. on September 6, Hurricane Irma made landfall on the sleepy island of Barbuda. By the time she left its leeward shore, 180 mph winds had devastated the sea-level territory of 1,700 souls, destroying most of the structures on the island. Two days later, the population would be evacuated to neighboring Antigua as Barbuda was surrendered to nature.

Later that morning, Irma dealt major damage to Saint Barts before reaching the French and Dutch island of Saint Martin. Her winds were at peak intensity as the eye passed directly over the island, damaging or destroying ninety percent of the buildings and causing widespread flooding. A year later, the Princess Juliana airport would still be operating out of tents.

To the south, the other two SSS Islands, Saba and Statia, were struck by the outer bands of the hurricane, the powerful winds tearing off roofs and stripping leaves from the trees. On Statia, The Quill was denuded of much of its foliage.

From there, Irma ripped into the U.S. and British Virgin Islands before visiting her fury on Puerto Rico, whipping up thirty-foot waves and dishing out a billion dollars in damage. The next day she smashed into the Turks and Caicos Islands, before brushing the Bahamas and angling toward Cuba. Irma weakened to a Category 2.

Turning north and strengthening to a Cat 4, she barreled into the Florida Keys, coming ashore at Cudjoe Key with 130 mph winds and a substantial storm surge. Much of the Middle and Lower Keys were devastated. Irma continued north into Florida, spawning numerous tornados and leaving eighty-four dead in that state alone, before roaring into the Southeastern U.S. to eventually die out in a deluge of rain.

When it was over, 134 people were dead and damage to property and infrastructure reached sixty-five billion dollars. Hurricane Irma broke multiple records, maintaining maximum sustained winds for a phenomenal length of time, and was recorded as one of the most powerful Atlantic hurricanes in history. And, as if that wasn't enough, Hurricane José was over the horizon with Hurricane Maria hot on its heels.

———— ◆ · ◆ ————

But back on Saba, on the morning of September 6, as Boone and Emily huddled together in the screaming dark at the top of Mount Scenery, the island below was experiencing the fury of the storm that lay just to the north. The movement of the storm's core meant the counter-clockwise spin of the swirling winds struck Saba from different directions throughout the morning. At first, the winds spun into the northwest coast near Well's Bay. Later, as Irma's eye moved west of Saint Martin, the winds came in on the west and south. Exposed on its bluff, St. John's was hit hard, numerous red roofs peeling off and flying down into the nearby guts.

Maskehorne Hill protected Windwardside somewhat, but the nature of the geography resulted in several microbursts being whipped up. This phenomenon was far worse in The Bottom, as multiple tornados and microbursts were generated in the bowl-shaped valley between the surrounding cliffs. All in all, on this five-square-mile island, some residents estimated that nearly two dozen tornados or near-tornados were generated, an astonishing number for such a small land mass. Unfortunately, one such tornado found Lucky's dive boat. *The Shoal 'Nuff* met her end as she was torn loose from the yard where she lay and dashed against a nearby retaining wall.

After the storm, residents recalled the wild events of those endless hours: some described their beds scooting across the floor, doors being pulled open, roofs peeled away, and everywhere, the disconcerting squeeze in the middle ear from the sudden drop in barometric pressure.

Miraculously, no one died on Saba during Hurricane Irma. Well ... *almost* no one.

———◆•◆———

The Servant opened his eyes—for all the good it did him. He could see nothing but dark shapes whipping by and the only sound he heard was the deafening roar of the wind, so loud it rivaled a

27

"Time is it?" a lump in the sleeping bag mumbled.

"No idea," replied the neighboring lump.

"Is it over?"

"Hope so." Boone shifted in the warmth of their cozy cocoon, stiffening at the jolt of pain in his side. "Ow. Wait! What if this is the eye of the hurricane?"

"I don't think so," Emily said. "The speed Irma was moving, it should be past us by now."

"So ... do we go outside?"

"Let's give it a minute, yeah? I'm kinda cozy."

"Ditto." Boone brushed a kiss against her lips—an easy task, considering how tightly they were entwined.

"I wonder if there's some hurricane version of the mile-high club we could apply for membership in," Emily whispered.

"We'd never qualify. Not while I'm being held together with duct tape."

"Yeah, 'spose you're right. Put a pin in it, though."

The night and morning had been unending, the wind sustaining a near-constant howl for hours. Boone and Emily had clung to each other throughout the ordeal as objects struck the building, nearby trees cracked and popped, and the sounds of banging and creaking mere feet from where they lay had the couple concerned that the door or windows would be torn from the walls or that the tower might topple. But the sturdy little structure weathered the storm. At last the wind weakened, the rain slackened, and the sounds of flying debris finally ceased.

"Okay. Let's unzip," Boone reluctantly said.

"The sleeping b—"

"Yeah, the sleeping bag."

Slowly, they extricated themselves from the warm cocoon and rose to their feet, Boone a little less steadily than Emily. She slipped an arm around him, careful to avoid the wound across his ribs. Approaching the door, Boone tried to flip the deadbolt.

"Damn, you weren't kidding," he said through gritted teeth. "It doesn't want to turn."

"Step aside, mortal," Emily said, smacking his hand from the latch and opening the door with a brutal twist. "Would you like to push the door open? So you can say you helped?"

Boone chuckled and opened the door, but it came to a halt almost immediately. Shouldering it, he was able to shove aside the debris, mostly branches, that had blown up against the western wall of the building. As they stepped outside into the moderate drizzle, Emily gasped.

"It's like a bomb went off...."

All around them, portions of many of the mountaintop's trees had been sheared off, vegetation stripped of its leaves. Water pooled in several places, little lakes created by smaller pools being blown together by the winds. Above, the massive red-and-white communications tower seemed intact, though Boone could see some cables strung in nearby branches like decidedly unfestive Christmas garlands. The air was incredibly humid, and wisps of cloud blew about. He took several steps toward the trail and stopped, looking around.

"Where's…?" Boone began.

"Don't know."

"What was his name, again?"

"Aidan. Means fire."

"Think the wind and rain might've snuffed him out."

"I see what you did there. Nice." Emily's words were playful, but her expression was sober as she looked up and down the trail. "No way he could survive this."

"That being said…"

"Yeah, let's get the hell out of here. Can you walk?"

"Think so. Feeling better after such a restful sleep. Storm drowned out your snoring."

Emily slapped a flattened palm hard on his bare upper back. "Ow!"

"Ooh, got a nice hand print with that one. You want me to tape that up for you?"

"I'll live." They walked down to the trail and headed back toward the steps. Boone spied the rope Emily had used to rescue him, still tied to a tree on the edge of the slope. He was debating retrieving it when his bare foot pressed down on something that wasn't mud. Stooping, he plucked a small object from the muck. It was covered in grime and the cord was now gone, but he knew immediately what it was. The blue bead.

"Is that…?"

"I can't believe that shack is still standing," Emily said, as the little banana plantation came into view. "That's where I woke up."

"Boone! Emily!"

"Up here!" Boone shouted.

Finally, the two groups spotted each other. Sid and Sophie, as well as a pair of Royal Dutch Marines, were climbing the trail from below. A fifth person, a mustached man wearing camo pants and a *Duff Beer* ballcap, brought up the rear. This man's composite metal walking stick put the others' to shame, appearing to be a purpose-built trekking pole.

"You two filming a Tarzan movie?" Sid quipped, as the rescue party gawked at the sight of Boone and Emily: shirtless, bloodied, caked in mud—and, in Boone's case, barefoot.

"Yeah. Sorry, chaps, all the roles are taken," Emily shouted back, breaking into relieved laughter at the sight of her friends and the soldiers.

Sophie approached, the mirth in her face melting away as she spied Boone's taped-up side. "What happened up there?" she asked. "Are you hurt? Is that ... duct tape? And Emily, your face!"

"What, am I going a bit Elephant Man?" she asked, touching her tender cheek, which was swelling and discolored. "But you should see the other guy." She started to giggle.

"You'll probably need binoculars, though," Boone said.

Emily burst into laughter, tears streaming down her face. Boone joined in, grabbing at his side and wincing, as all the tension of the past twenty-four hours was translated into gales of laughter.

Sid and Sophie stared at the pair with bemused looks on their faces.

"Maybe they're in shock. Dehydration?" one of the marines mused in a low voice.

"No—" Emily gasped between laughs "—it's just how we are!"

"But seriously," Boone managed, not looking serious at all. "We're gonna need a hospital."

"If it's not too much trouble," Emily snickered, bringing herself back under control.

Boone noticed that the marines were not armed. "Hey, Sid, the killer … he kidnapped Emily and … well, let me skip ahead: he may still be up there. The man's name is Aidan."

"It means fire," Emily tittered.

"Will you stop that?"

"Can't."

Sid interrupted. "Blond male, six-foot-two, gray coveralls. Remnants of duct tape on wrists and ankles."

"Where…?" Boone began.

"Upper Hell's Gate. Homeowner thought a tree hit her roof. Found him in her backyard."

Boone and Emily finally sobered. "How did you know where to look for us?" Boone asked.

Sid gestured back down the trail. "A resident found Gerald and Gordon's car down in Rendez-vous along with Mrs. Beach's yellow Hyundai. He thought it was odd and the phones were still down, so he drove down to Windwardside and spotted my patrol car. Once I got up there and saw the cars, I remembered you were staying with Gerald and Gordon…" He looked at Emily. "Or *The Double Gs* … nice one, by the way."

Emily curtsied. "Thank you."

"And I put it all together when I found these in the back of Mrs. Beach's car." He pulled Emily's sunglasses from a shirt pocket and offered them to her.

"Oh, thank God!" She slid them on, her face breaking into a beatific smile. "I really like this pair."

The man in the Duff hat stepped forward and spoke in a pronounced Saban accent. "You sheltered in the tower building?"

"Yes," Boone said.

He nodded. "That's what I woulda done. You find the sleeping bags?"

Emily smiled at him, "Yes! Boone was upset you didn't have any beer in there, though. He's such an ungrateful wanker."

The man laughed. "You'd have to talk to the telecommunications people 'bout that." He stuck out a hand. "James Johnson. Most folks call me Crocodile. Probably on account of this." He tapped his side, where an enormous knife hung in its sheath.

The sight sparked Boone's memory. "Sid … the murder weapon for Statia and Saint Kitts was probably a machete. I disarmed the killer and threw it…" He thought a moment. "To the right of the building, if you're facing it."

"I'll track it down," Crocodile said. "Sid, all-you okay getting back with these two? I want to see how my mountain is doing."

"Of course," Sid said.

"Croc here built this trail and its 1,064 steps," Sophie said with a sense of Saban pride.

"Well, not *all* the steps," the man said with a grin. "Just *most* of them. Four times a day, up and down the mountain with a donkey, a hundred pounds each of cement and water. With 2,000 other workers, of course. Lately, I've been working on all the other trails on the island…." He looked up toward the summit, shrouded in clouds. "But now it seems I'll be back working on this one." He pointed his trekking pole up the slopes. "How'd it look up there, after?"

Boone told him.

Croc nodded as if he'd expected it. "Yeah, was afraid of that. This is the worst I've seen. But…" He gestured around them at the stripped trees. "All of this? If we get some good rain, then in maybe three, four months … it will all be green again."

"Boone and I'll be sure to do a few rain dances for you, then." Emily said.

Croc tipped his cap to them. "Well, I'd better get to it, then." He turned and trudged up the mountain.

"How did the villages do?" Boone asked. "We saw a lot of roofs off here and there."

"Could've been worse," Sophie said. "The winds were insane. Couple people swear there were tornados. We're still assessing damage."

"Anyone hurt?" Emily asked.

"There is one gentleman, Christopher Brady, who the neighbors can't find. He may have sheltered with another family, so hopefully he'll turn up. As for injuries, aside from *that*—" Sid pointed at Boone's side "—I haven't heard of any injuries thus far. What happened to you, anyway?"

"Remember that machete I mentioned?"

Sid whistled. "Let's get you down to the hospital, then. I think they'll have something a little more professional than duct tape."

"Don't let Florence Nightingale hear you say that."

"You want another handprint on your back, beanpole?" Emily threatened with a grin.

"Come on," Sophie said, heading back down the slope. "Let's get you two down from here."

Shoal 'Nuff ... well ... total loss, I'm afraid. I mean, to be honest, she wasn't in the greatest shape to begin with..."

"I'm sorry, Lucky."

"Yeah. So ... here's the thing ... I know you left Bonaire to come here to work for Scenery Scuba, but ... Well, no easy way to say it: I'm gonna be shutting down for a while. The boat was insured, so I can afford to pay you for a bit. Maybe get your help cleaning things up. Shop took some damage. I may try again, I may not, but I'm afraid, for the foreseeable future..."

"Hey, Lucky, it's okay. And again, I'm sorry about your boat."

"Me too," Emily added.

Lucky looked like he might tear up but he quickly brightened. "Aw hell, I came here on a whim, I may *stay* on a whim. Who knows, maybe in a few months I'll come lookin' for you. *Both* of you." He jerked a thumb back toward the door. "If you'll excuse me a minute, I gotta go break the news to Chad."

"Well ... so ... *that* happened," Emily said, after Lucky left. "You think Frenchy would take us back?"

"Who's Frenchy?" Anika asked.

"Frenchy the Belgian," Boone said. "He owns the Bonaire dive shop we were working at, Rock Beauty Divers."

"Once the internet's up, I can drop him an email," Emily began. "I'm sure he'd—"

"Em ... I dunno."

Emily stopped, looking at him.

"This whole experience, dropping into a completely different place on the spur of the moment ... with you ... I loved it. I'm not sure I *want* to go back there just yet. Do you?"

"But ... we kinda need jobs, Boone. Jobs bring money, money brings food, food keeps you alive..."

"I've got a fair amount saved. You know me—I'm not a big spender."

"Yeah, but—"

"Umm ... excuse me?" Anika shyly raised her hand.

"Floor recognizes Anika," Emily said.

"Well ... just the day before yesterday, I received an email from a friend I went to school with. She's with a dive op that just moved to a bigger location and bought a new boat and they're searching for new dive instructors."

Boone and Emily looked at each other, a silent agreement passing between them.

"So ... if you're interested...?"

Boone reached for Emily's hand as he smiled at Anika. "What island?"

AFTERWORD

wanted to do something a little different in this afterword. Yes, I've got oodles of thank yous to dole out and they'll be along shortly. But first … this is a work of fiction. Now, one of the things I enjoy in my writing is the research, and I strive for accuracy when depicting a place. That being said, I certainly took a few liberties in this book and I thought it might be fun to let you all in on some of them. So, if you'd rather not "peek behind the curtain", then skip ahead!

First: Caribbean Reef Sharks. Attacks on divers by "reefies" are *extremely* rare. I did hear they had begun displaying a little aggression around some lionfish culls, but my scene with Chad was entirely fiction, a scene that popped into my head when I was diving a Saba site that had four or more of the beautiful creatures. I tried to mitigate some of the sensationalism of that scene by having Lucky pull up the International Shark Attack file to find out how rare attacks actually are. So … when you see a "reefy," sit back and enjoy the graceful creature. It isn't going to bother you.

The airport: Why did I place a WinAir Twin Otter on the cover headed toward the airport from the southeast when ninety-nine percent of flights will come from the northwest? Because it looked cool. Also ... I wanted you to better see the Hell's Gate side of the island as well as the famous airstrip, and Saba Tourism was kind enough to provide me with a marvelous photo to use on the cover. Also ... I got the rights to a fantastic shot of the exact type of plane that would be used, courtesy of an excellent photographer and airport enthusiast, Rolf Jonsen. Full disclosure: that plane is diving down to land at St. Barts, not Saba. Finally, pilots *do* sometimes land from that direction, if the winds require it. And since Boone and Captain Every were coming over from Statia ... "doing the triangle," which they don't do much anymore, I figured that was another reason they might come in from that angle.

Volcanoes: Just to be clear ... Saba is not going to blow anytime soon, probably not during our lifetimes, or our children's lifetimes. But where's the fun in *that*, if the Servant thinks this? Saba is very quiet, geologically. Although, I did stick my hand under the warm sand at the Hot Springs dive ... and felt the intense heat in a deeper part of The Sulphur Mine ... so it's easy to let the imagination run wild.

Dive sites: The nautilus shell that Chad shows off. Fact: It is a lawn ornament and it exists. Got some great photos of it and baffled my divemaster until Sea Saba told me what it was. Fiction: It's actually at the Ladder Labyrinth dive site, not Hot Springs. Another liberty I took: the Customs House dive is not typically done as a night dive but, for obvious reasons, I needed that to be the location. The next nearest site, Porites Point, wouldn't have a view of the customs house up on the cliff.

Over to the island of Sint Eustatius, or "Statia": I've been there twice—much of the content in the chapters set there is a reliving of some old memories. I am sad to report that Win, the German owner of the Kings Well, has passed away. I decided to keep him in the book. It was from him that I got my very own Statian Blue Bead. And the Smoke Alley was closed by the time of Irma, but I liked the location and chose to bend reality to the whims of my fiction. Statia is such an undiscovered gem and Boone and Emily will probably find themselves back there someday.

And here's a little fact-versus-fiction throwback: in *Deep Shadow*, I mention a KMar police boat operating between Saba and Statia. Well, on my trip to Saba to research this book I spoke to a KMar officer (KMar is a branch of police of the Dutch armed forces) and he said they didn't really have their own boat for that, but used the Dutch Caribbean Coast Guard instead. So that's why the cutter *Puma* had to be brought in.

Hurricane Irma: This hurricane dealt significant damage to numerous islands in the Leewards, no doubt about it, and it was record-breaking in its strength. But, of the 134 deaths attributed to Irma, ninety-two of them were actually in the United States. No one died on Saba or Statia. All things considered, Saba weathered the storm with minimal damage and was back up and running in an incredibly short period of time. Electricity was restored in twenty-four hours, communications shortly thereafter, and the entire island went out and cleaned everything up. An interesting bit of irony … later that month another Category 5 storm, Maria, swept into the Leewards. Her winds largely missed Saba but it gave them twenty-three inches of rain. Remember what Croc said about how it would all be green again if they got good rain? He actually said words to that effect, in a video taken just after Irma. And sure enough, when I visited the following year, ten months after Irma, the foliage was lush and green. The rain of a second hurricane helped repair the damage from the winds of the first.

In the interests of the book, I certainly hyped the storm ... although, to hear some of the stories from the Sabans who lived through it, I may not have done it enough justice. I was just looking at my notes as I write this afterword and one resident up on The Level said their winds were estimated at 225 mph! (this individual inspired the idea for the whistles, which they distributed throughout the household when the winds became terrifying). And the seismometer on Guadeloupe picking up Irma ... sounds really awe-inspiring, right? Actually, it's quite common for that to happen when a hurricane approaches.

And now for some hefty thank yous! I and my scuba buddies visited Saba in June 2018 and I was able to pack in a surprising number of interviews and tours to help with the research of this book. First and foremost, Sea Saba is without a doubt one of the best ops I've had the pleasure to dive with. Great boats, great dive instructors, and a well-appointed shop. Lynn and Mel at Sea Saba were fantastic (and both beta read this book, making sure I didn't make a hash of describing their island paradise). They seemed to know nearly everything I asked, and if they didn't know, they'd call someone who did. Thanks to Steve Knight, a dive instructor at Sea Saba, who gave me great insights into free diving and shallow water blackouts.

Ryan Espersen, an archaeologist at the Saba Heritage Center, took time out of two busy days to sit down with me over Long Haul pizza, regaling me with a dazzlingly diverse number of historical facts, before taking me and my mates all the way down into the old sulphur mine—I can't thank you enough! Tricia, up at Scout's Place, for some great information about Hell's Gate (and the Passionfruit Martini was excellent), Garvis Hassell and James "Steady Peddy" Johnson, two multi-generational Saban taxi drivers who gave me a phenomenal amount of useful tidbits about the people and culture on the island. Thanks to Andries and Eva of El Momo cottages for the jaw-dropping tale of your experience during Irma. The idea of holding the bathroom door shut against the wind haunted me. A big thank you to all the Saba Lace ladies who spent some time educating me about their art of "Spanish Lace" as well as recounting various experiences of the hurricane. A big thank you to Will Johnson. Will invited me up to his beautiful cottage on The Level and I chatted with him on his porch for a long while about all sorts of things. The cow kicking the seismometer? That was his anecdote. The unofficial historian for Saba, Will was a senator and governor ad interim on Saba for nearly forty years and has accumulated a mind-boggling amount of records and historical photographs, many of which can be seen on his website: www.thesabaislander.com. He's also an author! Alas, I was never able to catch a moment with the legendary James "Crocodile" Johnson—hardly surprising, as he really is out in the wild, keeping the astonishing trail system in good order. Guess I'll just have to go back.

Over on the island of Statia, thanks to the new owners of the Golden Rock Dive Center, Sarah and David, who were kind enough to answer some questions about the current state of the island. I have a special affection for the shop, as it is where I first learned to dive, taking lessons from the previous owner, Glenn Faires. In the interests of symmetry, when it was time to get an advanced certification, I did it there too. I was sad to hear that their building by Ro Ro pier was destroyed (sending them to a nearby temporary location) but I'm very pleased to learn that the original location will soon return! Thanks also to Win and Laura at the Kings Well. My visit with them is a bittersweet memory.

Thank you to all of my beta readers: Lynn Costenaro, Melanie Marks, Chris Sorensen, John Brady, Dan Sharkey, Peter Johnson, Dana Vihlen, Drew Mutch, Mike Ramsey, and James Cleveland. You all kept me accurate and helped me to flesh out a few plot points (and strip down some others). Thank you to Terence Zahner from the Saba Diving booth at the Beneath the Sea Expo for the information on birding in Saba ... sorry about what I did to the birdwatcher. And a special thank you to Angela Church, for allowing a certain Yorkipoo to make her fiction debut.

A *huge* thank you to Saba Tourism and Cees Timmers of TVC Advertising for the gorgeous photo of Saba, Rolf Jonsen for the dynamic photo of the plane, Shayne Rutherford of Wicked Good Book Covers for yet another beautiful cover, Marsha Zinberg of The Write Touch for her on-point editing, Colleen Sheehan of Ampersand Book Interiors for her excellent formatting, Kristie Dale Sanders for her chapter header of the Saba silhouette, and Gretchen Tannert Douglas and Sondra Wolfer for their keen-eyed proofreading skills and suggestions.

Thank you to ACX and Audible studios. It was my decades of narrating audiobooks that led me to try my hand at writing, and though there are numerous other studios I can thank for many of those books, it was the symbiosis of narrator and author through ACX that led to conversations with specific authors and finally set me on that path. And ... on that note...

A huge thank you to Wayne Stinnett and Michael Reisig, two phenomenal action adventure writers who have given me sage advice, encouragement, and support. When I say "I wouldn't be here without them," there isn't an ounce of hyperbole in the assertion.

Thank you to all the readers who read my first book. Many of you reached out to me and shared your own experiences under the sea and in the islands. Rest assured, I was taking notes.

And finally, I said it in the dedication to the last book, and I'll say it again here: thank you to Mom and Dad, for taking me to the Caribbean many times when I was young. You gave me a mask, snorkel, and "flippers"—yes, we called them flippers back then, so sue me—and I spent day after day with my eyes under the surface, discovering the wonders of our oceans. Beats Disney World.

ABOUT THE AUTHOR

Born in East Tennessee, Nick Sullivan has spent most of his adult life as an actor in New York City, working in theater, television, film, and audiobooks. After recording hundreds of books over the last twenty years, he decided to write his own. Nick is an avid scuba diver and his travels to numerous Caribbean islands have inspired this series.

For a completely different kind of book, you can find Nick Sullivan's first novel at:

WWW.ZOMBIEBIGFOOT.COM